THE ADVE~~NTURES OF~~

COBASFANG

JUSTICE RETURNS

Second Edition (Volume 1)

BY DAVID E. WALKER

THE ADVENTURES OF COBASFANG JUSTICE RETURNS SECOND EDITION (VOLUME 1)

Cobasfang Justice Returns first addition, was originally published by Page Publishing, Inc. 2018
Copyright © 2018 by David E Walker

Page Publishing Inc. New York, NY
ISBN 978-1-64214-457-4 (Paperback)
ISBN 978-1-64214-456-7 (Digital)

The Adventures of Cobasfang Justice Returns
Second Edition (Volume 1)

Copyright © 2021 by David E Walker
ISBN 978-1-7367955-3-8   (Hard Cover)
ISBN 978-1-7367955-4-5   (Paperback)
ISBN 978-1-7367955-5-2   (E-Book)

Printed in The United States of America

MY DEDICATION

With my deepest gratitude, I wish to shout to the world from the bottom of my heart, thank you.

To my family, to the ones that stand by my side when things are uncertain and life has become a struggle. For standing behind me even when the path I am blazing is running in a circle, and for standing in front of me and leading the way when I am overwhelmed and lost my way. But most of all, for giving me the courage to be myself.

To my parents, who were able to raise six kids without losing their minds or one of us in the store. (namely, me, running straight for sporting goods and the toy section) Trust me, at one time they had six teenagers, two dogs, and a whole lot of crazy times bouncing off the walls.

To the Baltimore Science Fiction Society and its insightful observations, I was finally able to polish my dreams and turn them into reality.

Without a doubt, I would like to give you my deepest gratitude for taking my dream into your life. Now it's time to let the creatures that filled the halls of my imagination to cross the boundaries of time and space and into your world. Enjoy!

TABLE OF ACTION

CHAPTER 1
THE JOURNEY BEGINS

From the moment a child is born, their precious life will swing beneath the tender threads of their choices. Most choices are made with little thought or concern, while the treacherous ones will twist the reality that binds their fate. Soon, Ty will realize how thin the web is that binds his soul to life when he decides to take matters into his own hands and enter the Forbidden Shadow Forest.

To tell you the truth, I'm not quite sure how to begin telling you about his incredible journey. So, I guess since this whole story is about Ty, I'll just take a second to tell you a little bit about him before we begin. So if you are ready, just sit back and relax, but you better hold on tight because the incredible journey one boy went through might change your life too.

His full name is Tyler, but since everybody calls him Ty,

we will too. He has deep brown eyes with short hair, and he's about your age. Now Ty lives with his Mom and Dad, grandmother, and his little brother Bob. He spends most of his time at home with his brother playing video games and loves going fishing with his Dad whenever they get a chance. But when he gets out of school, he likes to go bike riding with his best friends, Dylan and Xavier, or go exploring in the fields on the outskirts of town next to the barricade. But sometimes, when there's nothing much to do, Ty will just hang out in the tree fort and read some comic books.

This wild adventure of Ty's started early on a warm and sunny Saturday morning at the beginning of summer. Xavier, Dylan, and Ty were all hanging out inside the tree fort they built at the end of the street behind old man Grady's house. It was the strongest fort in town. Ty, Dylan, and Xavier made it out of some old lumber they scavenged from the lumberyard across town. It had a thick, sturdy door and two windows made from the doors off an old washer and dryer. Its roof was made out of an old blue tarp he got from his uncle, and it would flap when the wind blew hard through the tree. They had a table and three old folding chairs, but one of the coolest things this fort had was a secret trapdoor hidden beneath a rug under a rope hammock in the corner.

Now Ty, Xavier, and Dylan were all sitting inside playing cards when Bob came bursting up through the trapdoor, crying and yelling his head off for Ty.

"What your problem, Bob?" Ty snapped as he leaned back on his chair. "You know you can't come in until you knock!"

"Ty, I think Dad's hurt! I just saw Uncle John carrying Dad down the street, headed back home. C'mon, Ty. Let's go."

"What do you mean Dad's hurt? Just go back home, and I'll be right behind you."

Just as Bob slipped through the trapdoor, Dylan looked out the window. "I don't see your Dad. Do you want us to go with you, Ty?"

"No, I don't know. Guys, I've gotta go. But I'll meet you at the pond after dinner if you wanna go fishing."

Then tossing his cards on the table, Ty slipped out through

the trapdoor and scurried down the tree. But when he ran around old man Grady's pool, he saw Bob in the front yard being picked on by the neighborhood bullies Pete and Joe. They had him pinned against a tree real hard and shoving a long black snake in his face.

Those two jerks were two years older and a lot bigger than Ty, and they were always in trouble. Whenever something went wrong or someone got in trouble, you always heard their names shouted out first.

"Stop squirming, you little twerp," shouted Joe as he tried to shove it down his shirt. "Or I'll make you eat it."

"Hey! What's going on?" shouted Ty as he ran up to those two bullies. "Leave my brother alone!"

As Ty grabbed Joe's arm and tried to rip the snake out of his hands, Pete grabbed Ty by his shirt and slammed him to the ground. "After we take care of your little brother, you're next!" shouted Pete as he sat on Ty's chest.

"Leave me alone," screamed Bob as Joe tried to uncoil that snake from around his arm.

The rage inside Ty started to boil as he watched Bob kicking and screaming for help. Ty wasn't gonna take it anymore as he gritted his teeth then slugged Pete right in the mouth as hard as he could. That solid smack sent both of them rolling across the yard and into the deep, muddy ditch, swinging and punching on the way down.

After a few seconds, Ty managed to get Pete in a headlock and started squeezing tight as Joe went flying into the ditch and crashed on top of them with a huge thud.

"What the heck?" Muttered Ty as he looked up and saw Xavier and Dylan standing at the top of the ditch with their hands on their hips.

"Get out of here right now, or we are gonna bust you two up!" shouted Dylan as he kicked a clump of mud at Pete.

Those bullies knew they were outnumbered and they took off running down the block, but when they passed Ty's house, you could hear Joe screaming back at them, "This ain't over! We're gonna get you for that."

"Thanks, guys," Ty grumbled while crawling out of that ditch. "Those two are going to get it for messing with my little brother!"

"Are you ok, Bob?" Ty muttered as he stood up and brushed the mud off his pants, "You gotta get over being afraid of snakes; they can't hurt you. Now come on, let's get back home. Ok?"

Ty rubbed the top of Bob's head then grabbed his hand as they started running back home. But just as they got close to their front yard, Bob took one look up at Ty and bolted for the door. He was running so fast that he nearly knocked his Mom down as she tried to hold the door open.

"What happened to you and your brother young man? You're all muddy, and you're making a mess in my living room," she snapped as she slammed the door behind them.

"Sorry, Mom," shouted Ty as he ran into the kitchen. "We're at the fort playing cards with Dylan and Xavier, and I fell in the ditch by Mister Grady's house. What happened to Dad?"

"Your father got hurt at Eagle Cliff again, digging for some blue fire rubies for Grandma. He should know better than that. Those tunnels near the northern cavern are too dangerous, and they're unstable. Just like your father!"

"Unstable or not, Marie, that's where you have to dig. If you had the slightest clue about geology, you'd know that!" Ty's Dad winced as he leaned back on the couch. "We had to dig pretty deep through a vein of iron ore when John spotted a small cluster growing out from behind a large chunk of bedrock. We dug as hard as we could when the walls started to collapse! Those old timbers we used to shore up the tunnel started snapping like toothpicks. John and I barely got out with our lives, and just as we dove out of the cave, a timber came hurling out and hit me in the leg. I think it's broke."

"Tyler, go and get my bag from downstairs," ordered Marie as she walked back into the room. "And John, would you go into the kitchen and grab the small blue bowl under the counter and fill it halfway with soap and water so I can clean this leg off and get a better look? There's a clean washcloth in the drawer next to the sink. Grab one of the green ones, not my good white ones."

Ty's Mom just happened to be the best doctor in town, and she knew right away that his Dad's leg didn't look too good. She put her coffee down on the end table then bent down to get a good look. She very carefully examined his injured leg and could see right away; it was broken.

"Well Cobias, the winds of luck must have been with you today. It looks like you only have a hairline fracture," she snickered softly as she stood back up. "But don't worry, it won't take me long to put a cast on it. But I'm afraid that you're gonna have to use crutches for at least six weeks."

"Yeah, I know," he sighed as he grabbed a quick sip of her coffee. "But at least it wasn't a total disaster. Before the cave collapsed, John was able to grab a small chunk from that cluster of rubies, and I grabbed three nice pieces of blue fire rubies from the south tunnel."

While John cleared off a spot on the table to put the bowl of soapy water down, Marie took a look at what they brought home.

"Those are some really nice ones, and they have a powerful glow. But I'm afraid it's not gonna be enough. They're just too small," she replied softly as she placed them on the table. "Now If I mix them with some papa root, I might be able to make just enough to make Grandma feel a lot better for a couple more days. Honey, I'm gonna need a lot more just as strong as these if I'm going to have a chance to help her."

(I guess I forgot to tell you about blue fire rubies. You see, they get their name because of the warm mystical glow that swirls around them when the light is dim or when a storm approaches. You can tell how old they are by how deep the fire grows when you hold them in your hands. But the reason why they are so valuable is that when a true crystal healer makes potions out of them, they can heal all kinds of injuries or even cure diseases. Nowadays, the only place left that you can find these gems is deep inside the caves at Eagle Cliff, and if those old stories are true, you might find some in the caves hidden deep within the Shadow Forest! Nobody really knows for sure, because in the last two hundred years, no one has ever made it out of there alive.)

While Ty's parents were trying to figure out how to get their hands on some more blue fire rubies, Ty ran back upstairs and placed the medical bag on the table next to his Mom. "Is Dad going to be ok?" Ty whispered to his Mom so his Dad couldn't hear.

"He'll be fine," she replied with a little smile. "Now get out of those muddy clothes right now. Your sisters, Cristan and Kelly are coming over to visit later, and we'll be eating soon, so if you go anywhere, don't be late, or you'll miss lunch again."

Ty gave her a quick nod then raced upstairs to his room to change. But as soon as he shoved the door open, he saw Bob sitting on his bed, still shaken up from what those bullies tried to do. Then sitting down next to Bob, he gave him a little nudge and whispered softly with a sneaky smirk, "Don't you worry about those jerks. I'll make sure they never mess with you again!"

Bob stood up and threw a pillow across the room, knocking an empty cup off Ty's dresser, trying to look tough. "I'm not afraid of them. I was just scared that the snake would eat me!"

Ty just smiled and tossed him his signed baseball cap. "I'll teach you all about snakes so you'll never be scared of them anymore. Ok? Now tell Mom I'm going fishing at the river and I might spend the night at Dylan's house. Oh yeah! Mom said don't forget to wash your hands before you come down."

Trying not to get caught again for ditching lunch, Ty crawled out the window and headed down his secret trail to the edge of the lake. As soon as he got there, Ty sat down in his favorite spot on the old tree stump next to the great pit and just leaned back and started to toss a few rocks in. He knew he wasn't allowed to hang out over there, but that never stopped him before. The only time he went over there was when he wanted to do some serious thinking or when he got really bored. But sometimes Xavier and Dylan would show up, and they would throw rocks into the great pit just to see if they could hear one hit the bottom. Last year, Dylan swore that he tossed a huge rock down there and heard a ghostly squeal come up from the depths of that deep, dark hole. Nobody really knew how deep it was because nobody was ever stupid enough to climb down there, not even Pete and Joe.

While he sat there, Ty just couldn't stop thinking about what his Mom said about his grandma, and he knew that his Dad wouldn't be able to get any more healing rubies now that he had a broken leg. He wanted to do something to help save his grandma, and since his Dad couldn't do anything with a broken leg, he figured it would be up to him to find some more.

With the caves by Eagle Cliff destroyed, the only other place he figured he could find some would be deep within the Shadow Forest. However, the thought of going into that place scared him so much that he nearly threw up. Ty knew the creatures that lurked in the Shadow Forest were ten times worse than any nightmare you could ever have. In history class, he learned that there were mystical witches so powerful that they could capture you in a blink of an eye and feast on your bones for a hundred years. Sometimes at night, when the air was calm and the night mist crawled across the ground. Ty and his brother would sneak out of their house and sit on the edge of their roof and listen to their nightmarish howling echoing out from the depths of those forbidden woods.

This is why the grown-ups where Ty lives surrounded their village with towering rows of razor bushes. Now everybody knows that razor bushes are nothing to mess with. Their silvery leaves are about the size of a bottle cap and are sharper than any razor blade ever made. Sometimes, in the cold dim light of the moons, Ty could see the leaves shimmering with an eerie green glow from his bedroom window. Those razor bushes are the perfect thing to protect his village from the nightmarish creatures that creep in those woods. Just the slightest brush against the smallest leaf will slice even the most savage monster to the bone.

As Ty sat there tossing rocks in the pit, all he could think about was how badly his grandmother needed those blue fire rubies. He knew that if his Mom found out what he was planning to do, she would lock him up in his room and throw away the key.

So he figured he had no other choice as he slowly stood up and looked over to the edge of the shadow forest, and took a deep breath. He knew that if he was going to do this, he would have to go now. Because if he went home and grabbed the things he'd need, his Mom would figure out what he was planning to do in a second and stop him cold.

So Ty just stood there for a moment and started to get a sneaky, sinister little smile and thought, "I can do this, no problem, I'll zip in fast then get out." With uneasy confidence, he brushed the dirt off his pants and figured he might as well get started. Then with a deep breath, he gathered up some courage and boldly started walking across the field, heading straight for the Shadow Forest. The tall thistle grass was swaying back and forth as a bone-chilling wind swept down from the mountain. "This ain't good," he thought to himself as some goosebumps crawled up his arm, but he just clenched his teeth and kept on walking further away from home.

When he got a bit closer to the edge of the forest, a ghostly mist began to rise up from the ground and swept across his feet. Ty froze right where he was and realized there was absolutely no way he would go in there unarmed. So, he started looking around to see what kind of weapon he could come up with as he walked through the field.

Now Ty was a smart kid, but there was nothing in that field except for some old jagged rocks and thistle grass. "Wait just a minute," he mumbled as he started to grin and looked by his feet. "This might work quite nicely."

Ty reached down and picked up a couple of flat skipping stones and started chipping away at the sides of those rocks just like the great Indians used to do. Before long, he made himself a very sharp knife and some real cool arrowheads. Then the moment Ty got close to the edge of the forest. He grabbed the straightest and strongest stick he could find and made himself a spear!

Next, he used the cord from his jacket hood and a sturdy branch from a hickory tree he found on the ground to make an extra-strong bow. He was almost ready to enter those dangerous woods with arrows made from solid oak and razor-sharp arrowheads of stone. The last thing he needed was something to hold all the arrows he made. But as he was looking around, he figured there was only one thing he could do. So, he ripped off the sleeves of his sweatshirt and used that as a quiver to keep his arrows tight and secure.

Of course, Ty was still a bit scared, but who could blame him? He was planning to go in the Shadow Forest alone, armed only with a handful of arrows, a spear, and a knife made of stone. Making weapons strong enough to protect himself wasn't the only problem he had to solve. The biggest problem he had to figure out was how he was getting past the razor bush barricade in the first place.

So, he started walking along the tall barricade, trying to find any place big enough to squeeze through until he spotted a long tree branch that fell across it and smashed it flat. "This must be my lucky day," he boasted out loud as he zipped over the branch like a cat. But Ty knew he had to get his bearings before he went any further. The forest was so thick with trees and bushes he couldn't see very far at all. So Ty started looking for the tallest tree he could climb to get a good look around. That was when he saw it. Just up ahead on top of the hill was the biggest tree he had ever seen in his life—an enormous oak tree growing right out of a massive pile of boulders.

I don't know about you, but I think doing some boulder hopping and climbing trees is almost as much fun as jumping your bike off ramps into Jason's pond, and Ty thought so too.

So Ty took off and started running as fast as he could. Weaving his way around some thick bushes, then sprinting up the hill, he made it to the pile of boulders in just a couple of minutes. Then with one gigantic leap after another, Ty pounced and lunged from one jagged boulder to the next until he reached the base of that mighty oak tree.

Ty looked up and smiled because it looked like it would be a lot of fun to climb. So he jumped up as high as he could, grabbed onto the lowest branch, and swung into action. It was a perfect climbing tree! Each branch was so close it was almost like climbing a ladder. Ty was having so much fun hopping from branch to branch he didn't even notice when they started to pop and creak the higher he climbed. In no time at all, he had to begin squirming and wiggling between the branches as he neared the top, and that's when Ty had his first good look at the Shadow Forest below.

It was the most beautiful thing he ever saw. The forest looked like a green wave of trees, flowing across the land like an ocean and splashing against the mountains in the distance. As Ty sat there looking at the forest below, he spotted something quite incredible. There was a magnificent mountain sparkling and glittering in the distance as if it was created with diamonds. Now that looked like a perfect place to find what he was after.

"This is going to be easier than I thought." Ty chuckled as he started to climb back down.

Then about halfway, Ty heard a strange noise coming from the heart of the forest. It was a low rumbling and crashing sound, getting closer and closer. Suddenly, the whole tree he was in started to rock back and forth from the shockwaves of those frightening sounds. Ty held his breath, trying as hard as he could not to make a sound, as he strained to see what was coming. But it didn't take long before he got a glimpse of something that sent shivers down his back. He couldn't believe his eyes as he watched two large horn-backed bears burst out of the woods like scared little rabbits.

"What in the heck would those things be so afraid of?" Ty thought to himself as he stared into the field below. That was when he saw what they were so afraid of: it was a gigantic rinog lumbering out of the shadows of the forest and stepping into the clearing

If you never heard of a rinog before, let me tell you. They are the most ferocious creatures alive, and they're known worldwide for being the worst-tempered creature on the planet. As you might imagine, a rinog has a head like a rhino and club-like hands, and their hide's so tough no spear ever made can penetrate it. This huge monster had to be at least ten feet tall from the tip of its pointy gray horns to the ground. Ty took one look at the weapons he had and knew that he would be a goner if that thing saw him. So he clung onto that tree as hard as he could, not moving a muscle.

While he held on to that branch as hard as he could, he started whispering a prayer that the beast couldn't hear the sound of his heart pounding in his chest. The woods instantly went quiet, the crickets stopped chirping, and even the birds in the trees slipped deeper within their nests as it lumbered through the thick, tall grass. The clearing turned as quiet as a graveyard on a cold winter's night.

Just when the rinog walked beneath that mighty oak tree, a loud crack rang out from the branch Ty was clinging on to. A bead of sweat rolled down Ty's forehead as he peered down at the top of its head as it stood there grunting at the buzzing flies. The branch he was clinging on wasn't going to hold much longer. He knew he would be in real serious trouble if that rinog spotted him because that beast would crush his bones into dust.

With a chilling growl, it looked all around, trying to find out what made that noise. You could see the muscles rippling in its massive body as it scavenged through the boulders, searching for something to crush. Suddenly, it must have seen something lurking in the shadows deep within the woods because it took off running like a demon on fire. The ground shook like thunder as the trees smashed to the ground when it disappeared out of sight. Ty didn't even try to climb down until the ground stopped shaking and the crickets started chirping once again. That was way too close!

Ty leaned back, wiped the sweat from his brow, and finally exhaled. He admitted to himself the cold hard fact that if he wasn't more careful, he would never make it out of there alive. After sitting quietly for a moment, gathering his nerve, he reached up and grabbed the crooked branch above him to start climbing back down. But before he could get a good hold of it, the limb he was standing on snapped in half, sending Ty tumbling down toward the cold hard ground.

"Oh no!" screamed Ty. Smacking and slamming from branch to branch, Ty fell out of control through the tree. He tried as hard as he could to grab ahold of a branch to stop himself, but he was falling way too fast, and he was seconds away from smashing into the jagged boulders below.

"What should I do?" he thought in a panic as his jacket started flapping wildly in the wind. Then in a desperate move, Ty grabbed his stone knife and slammed it so hard into that tree's leathery trunk that it split open wide and stuck in deep. The ripping sounds of bark flying into the air bled from the tree as he began to slow down, saving him from splattering against the boulders below!

Dangling from only his fingertips around his knife, he used his last bit of strength to rip his blade free and jump onto the boulders below. He was still pretty scared and shaking uncontrollably on top of that cold and slippery boulder. Then after a few minutes of just sitting there and moaning and throbbing in pain, he lifted his shirt to see how badly scraped up his side was.

"That was way too close!" he thought as he slid his shirt back down. "I've gotta be more careful."

But that would be nothing compared to the trouble that lay ahead for our young hunter.

CHAPTER 2

THE VIPERCON ATTACKS

After Ty regained his strength, he hopped across the boulders and headed towards the Crystal Mountain. Ty figured the only way he was gonna stay alive would be to stay close to the trees, just in case that rinog returned. As he limped along the edge of the forest, he couldn't help noticing how the woods smelled kind of musty and stale, and the ground was thick with leaves, making it soft and spongy. The woods seemed to be crawling with all kinds of creatures. Everywhere he looked, from every dark crevice, eyes were watching him. It felt real spooky walking through those woods during the day, and he was afraid to imagine what it's going to be like when darkness came.

When Ty made it to the bottom of the next ravine, he had a wonderful surprise. It was a large sweet apple tree. 'What perfect timing," he thought while standing there staring at its bright red fruit. After all that walking, some delicious fresh apples would hit the spot. He looked around to make sure the coast was clear, ran up to it, then filled his arms with a dozen plump, ripe apples. He felt so proud of himself for making it all this way and finding some food gave him the confidence to keep ongoing. So he sat down in the cool shade of that apple tree, ate a few apples, and filled his pockets for a little snack later.

Ty was so desperate to find a cave in the Shadow Forest and get out with what he came for alive, he quickly jumped back up and started to make his way to the Crystal Mountain. At first, he crept slowly across the bottom of the ravine, trying not to make a sound as he made his way over mounds of loose rocks and rotting logs. But as Ty approached the other end of the ravine, he started to gag on the awful stench that swept across the ground like a thick green cloud. It was so bad he had to cover his mouth with his shirt as his eyes started to water.

Ty took a few minutes to keep from getting sick and then crawled over an old moldy willow tree lying at the edge of the ravine to get a better look. He couldn't believe what he saw. Up ahead was a disgusting swamp, bubbling with brown slime that exploded in orange flames as it popped on the surface. It was the nastiest thing he had ever seen in his life. There was no way on earth he was going to walk through that bubbling pool of sludge. But turning back now was not an option, so Ty had no choice. He had to find a way around that swamp.

Staying as far away from the mushy ground as he could, Ty started climbing through the thick bushes that grew along the side of the hill. As he struggled to make his way past a dead sticker bush, Ty spotted a creepy cave all covered with green moss. "Why not?" Ty thought. "This is as good a place as any to start looking for the blue fire rubies, and if I find some here, I won't have to go any further."

Ty was well aware of the dangers hidden deep inside of caves, so he held his spear tightly and walked in nice and slow. The first thing he found was a couple of green vampire bats hanging from the ceiling and all kinds of poisonous spiders crawling around its cold, damp walls. After flicking a couple of the bigger ones out of his way with the tip of his spear, he crouched down lower and kept on going. But there was something about this cave that didn't seem right. As he slowly made his way deeper into the cave, he started to hear the faint sounds of a few stones tumbling down the side of the cave's wall right in front of him. His heart started pounding in his chest; he knew that he wasn't alone.

Suddenly, Ty heard a soft voice whispering from deep from inside the cave. "Don't be afraid. Just come a little closer. You look like a tasty little snack."

Now as you've already seen, Ty was no fool, so he kept his spear ready and backed out of the cave in a hurry. Then standing outside on solid ground again with his spear held ready, Ty shouted as loud as he could, "Those are brave words coming from someone cowering inside a cave. Why don't you come out here and say that to my face if you dare?"

Ty stood there defiantly, staring into the blackness of the cave. "Well? What's wrong? Did you lose your appetite?"

That's when Ty spotted two green eyes as large as dinner plates slowly moving closer and closer to the opening of the cave. Ty took a step back, braced himself, and shouted out again, "I don't know who you are, but if you think you're gonna make me your snack, all I can tell you is you're right about to have a real bad day!"

Out of the shadows deep within the cave, Slowly slithered the biggest vipercon he had ever seen. (You might not know this, but vipercons are the most poisonous snake on the whole planet. If that isn't bad enough, they're famous for having big appetites and bad tempers.) This one looked to be about fifty feet long, with brownish spots swirling across its muscular scaly back. It slowly slithered out into the daylight and coiled up right in front of Ty.

"You look a little puny to have such a big mouth," it hissed as its head softly swayed side to side. "But I am hungry, so you'll have to do."

"I don't have time for this foolishness," shouted Ty as he puffed out his chest and slammed the butt of the spear deep into the ground. "So you better get back in your hole, or I'll

15 The Vipercon Attacks

make snake-skin boots for my whole family out of you!"

"How dare you talk to me that way!" hissed the vipercon, flicking his tongue in the air. "My bite is sharper than your words."

Quick as lightning, it snatched Ty right off the ground, wrapped its massive muscular body tightly around Ty, and slowly started to squeeze the life out of our young warrior. The more Ty struggled, the tighter it squeezed. Within seconds of being snatched up in that vipercon's mighty grip, His legs were starting to go cold and numb.

With a cold and heartless hiss, that vipercon muttered, "If you have anything else to say, you can say it in my stomach." It opened its huge blood-dripping mouth and lunged for the killing strike.

"I don't think so!" Ty shouted out loud and defiantly.

With a flick of his wrist, Ty reached up and snatched that thing by its fangs and pulled it up so close they were nose to nose. Then Ty took his spear and stuck it right between those two huge green eyes and boasted out loud, "Look here rat breath. You don't know who you're messing with, and I don't have time to teach you any manners. So if you don't put me down right now, I'll break this spear off in your head and leave you for the flies and maggots to feast on!"

"You're very brave for such a little thing," it said in a soft and teasing voice, "or very stupid! Either way, you speak with a sharp tongue. I have a sharp tongue too. Let's see how you like how sharp my tongue can be."

It flicked its tongue out and—smack! It slapped Ty across his face so hard his head flew back like he was hit with a hammer.

Ty let out a thunderous roar, shook his head, and slung that vipercon's spit in all directions. "You disgusting rat-filled worm, that's the grossest thing ever! But if you're really hungry, why don't you have an apple?" Just as fast as he could, Ty reached into his pocket and pulled out an apple, then stuck it on that vipercon's fang!

"How dare you!" it hissed furiously while trying to flick that apple off with his tongue. "I'll crush you for that!" Then it started to squeeze even harder. So hard, in fact, Ty thought his bones were beginning to crack.

"I warned you, rat breath! It seems like I'm gonna have to teach you a lesson." Looking deeply into those cold green eyes, he grabbed that fang, dripping with venom, and ripped it right out of the vipercon's mouth with an eerie pop!

"Youch! That hurts!" it screamed out in shock as it snapped its head back.

"If you want to live five seconds longer, you'd better put me down right now before I get really get mad and put that fang back in your head, pointy side first!"

With blood gushing out from its jaw, the vipercon slowly let Ty back to the ground. "You're a fearless little creature," it muttered as it spit some blood on the ground. "My name is Normack. Who are you?"

Ty tried as hard as he could to stand up straight, but his legs were numb and nearly crushed. So he stuck his spear into the ground and held on tightly. "My name is Ty, and I'm on a journey through these dark woods in search of blue fire rubies. There's a mountain on the other side of this swamp just west of here that sparkles like diamonds. I'm headed over there to find some."

"I've been to that place before, and it's a dangerous journey indeed. I can take you there safely if you want."

"Oh really?" laughed Ty aloud as he flicked more of his spit on the ground. "I don't believe you. Do you think I am stupid or something, and why should I trust you? You'll just try to eat me once my back is turned."

The vipercon rose straight up in the air and hissed with a booming voice, "Are you calling me a liar? If there's one thing about a vipercon you had better understand is that we do not lie. We do not trick or deceive. We're an honorable race, and our word is our bond! No creature has ever stood his ground to me and walked away. I owe you a debt of honor. I'll pay this debt to you by helping you find your treasures. I give you my word!"

Ty still thought this could be a trick, but he figured it would be better to travel next to this vipercon where he could keep an eye on him than to worry about it sneaking up from behind.

"Sure, I'd enjoy some company, but if this is some kind of trick and you try to eat me again, you'll be sorry you ever came out of your cave!"

"I won't ever try to eat you again, young master," Normack replied as he shook his head. "To tell you the truth, you tasted worse than fish feet rotting in a pool of swamp sludge!"

"Very funny, especially coming from someone whose breath smells like wet rat butt."

They both started to laugh so hard that they couldn't breathe! It looked like Ty had made himself a friend out here in the Shadow Forest.

After Normack stopped laughing, he told Ty, "If you want to go to the Crystal Mountain, then we must cross the swamp. There's a great place, not far up ahead, where we can safely swim across. The muck floating on top is thin and it won't drag you down."

"Are you nuts? You want to swim across this?" laughed Ty as he tried to cover his nose. "I wouldn't get in this bubbling sludge even if the woods were on fire. Anyway, I can't swim, so we have to find another way around."

"What do you mean you can't swim?" chuckled Normack while coiling up in front of him. "It's hard to believe how someone that tastes like a rotting fish's corpse can't even swim across one little puddle swamp. But don't worry, I know another way you can get across without getting your scales wet. Ten years ago, a tornado ripped through here like a demon and blew down an enormous willow tree. It was so huge it fell completely across. You might be able to use it as a bridge. That is if you have enough balance with those little feet of yours to walk across it."

"All right!" grumbled Ty as he pulled his spear out of the ground. "Let's get to the tree as fast as we can because if I have to smell this place any longer, I am gonna throw up."

Normack led the way through the thick brush covering the bank of the swamp. Smashing flat the twisted thorn bushes, he made a nice path for Ty to follow. It didn't take long until they made it to the tree bridge. (Let me tell you, it looked more like a floating pile of weeds than a tree.) But Ty knew if they didn't cross there, it would take days to walk all the way around that massive swamp.

"I'll go first," Ty said while giving one of its branches a little wiggle. "But we gotta go cross one at a time. I don't

18 The Vipercon Attacks

think this floating flytrap can hold the both of us."

Ty held his breath and cautiously started weaving around the rotting branches, trying desperately not to slip on the slimy wet moss. Every step he took, some gross black goop would start oozing up from what was left of the tree trunk. The further he went out, the deeper the tree began to sink. He could hear it pop and squish as he made his way across, but using his spear to keep his balance, he just kept on going, inch by inch.

When he made it to the dead rat that was floating in the bubbling muck, he knew he was getting closer to the other side. Then all of a sudden, Ty slipped on a slug and started to fall in backward. In a desperate move, he slammed his spear deeper into the tree, jumped back to get his balance, and held on for dear life! But his foot broke through the log and got jammed deep inside, trapping him as the tree started to pitch and rollover.

"Look out, Ty!" yelled Normack as he watched helplessly from the shore.

"No way am I going to fall in this mess!" screamed Ty as he held on as tight as he could. Bending and twisting his spear, he tried desperately to keep from falling in while it splashed and flung clumps of muck and ooze in all directions.

When it finally came to rest, Ty was still hanging on, holding his breath and shaking with fear.

"Are you all right?" Normack shouted as he rose as high as he could to see.

"Yeah, I'm ok," Ty said softly as he gave him a thumbs-up.

Then after taking a deep breath, he slowly started to pull his foot loose. But as soon as his foot popped loose, he felt something squirming around his ankle. That's when he looked down and saw dozens of giant bugs with hook-like pincers and scorpion-like tails come pouring out from the hole. They started crawling on his shoes and up his legs as he desperately tried to knock them off before they could swarm all over him. The more he struggled to knock them off, the more that log started to bounce and splash again. Ty knew that if he lost his balance this time, he would be going for a swim. He had to get off this floating pile of leaves fast, or he was going to be bug food. Frantically, Ty pulled out his spear and started to run.

Huge pieces of bark and branches were snapping off and flying in the air with every step he took. It was falling apart fast, and Ty was still pretty far from shore. It was all or nothing, so he started to run even faster. Suddenly, with a loud crack, the end of the tree snapped off and started to float away. With all the strength he had left, Ty dove for shore. A loud thud echoed across the swamp as he landed safely across!

"Nice moves," shouted Normack as he watched him crawl away from the shore and plop down on the gravel. "Nice moves, indeed!"

Slithering slowly across what was left of that tree, Normack made his way over to where Ty was sitting. As he looked down, he started to snicker. "With a jump like that, you must be part frog too."

"Are you kidding me? I could jump twice that far to avoid landing in that stuff. If you think you're so good, then I'll race you up the hill to the Crystal Mountain."

"Wait, stop right there. You can't go that way!" Shouted Normack as he slithered up to Ty. "You're headed straight for the land of the rock monster, Grog. If that thing finds us, it'll grind us into dust. It can't stand anything trespassing on its land. Even the birds aren't safe when they fly over that place."

After Ty's little adventure crossing that swamp, he didn't want to listen to anything Normack had to say. "Don't be such a sissy, Normack. This is the quickest way to the Crystal Mountain, and I'm not afraid of anything!"

"Ty, you have no idea what you are getting yourself into! There's nothing sissy about avoiding a place that'll put your life at risk! Knowing when to enter an area and when to avoid one is a sign of maturity. That's a lesson that you need to learn fast before your pride gets us both killed!"

"Whatever," Ty muttered as he started climbing up the hill. "I'm not going to let anything stop me from saving my grandma, but if it makes you feel better, we can sneak past those hills, staying in the shadows and keeping quiet. You're scary, scary little monster poo, Groggy, will never know we were ever there. So pull up your big boy scales, and let's get moving. It is a long way to that mountain, and I want to get as far away from this stinking pit as fast as I can!"

CHAPTER 3
THE MOUNTAIN IS ALIVE

Silently, they crept up the steep hill filled with thorn bushes and thick brush. Normack was a natural at stealth, and Ty traveled as quietly as a whisper. The only sound you could hear was the soft murmur of a cool breeze blowing down the valley and through the trees. As they continued on their journey, Ty and Normack slowly worked their way around to the edge of a sharp pile of boulders protruding up between two large evergreen trees at the top of the hill.

When Normack gently rose up to get a better look, he noticed something glittering up ahead. "What is that?" he whispered back to Ty as he flicked his tongue a few times.

"I'm not sure yet, but I think I might know what it is.

When we get to the top of the next hill, we should be able to get a better look."

As they snuck through the next valley, both Ty and Normack kept a sharp lookout for any sign of trouble. But when they got closer to the top of the next hill, Ty told Normack to wait behind a large grove of mulberry bushes, then crawled on his belly and peeked over the top of the hill. After a quick look, he crawled back to where Normack was and sat down with a disgusted look on his face.

"I was afraid of that. I was hoping I was wrong, but I know exactly what it is." Ty grumbled under his breath as he tossed a rock into the woods. "Those are razor bushes up ahead, and there's no way we'll be able to go that way. We have those bushes surrounding my village, and nothing can get through it without being sliced to ribbons. We've gotta find another way around."

"You make me laugh!" hissed Normack as he slithered across the ridge. "You're so eager to run through Grog's home turf, but you tremble at the sight of some weeds."

"I told you before. I'm not afraid of you or anything else in the forest." He shouted as he whipped another rock right at a tree. "But there's no way we'll ever make it across that stuff."

"Take it easy, fish feet. I can help you get across, but you must trust me."

"All right, but we have to move fast. I don't wanna get caught out in the open. Those bushes are a long way away, and there's nothing to hide behind. We'll have to cross a pretty big field before we get there. If you're ready, we'll make a break for it. Ready, set, go!"

In a flash, those two took off racing across the field. Ty tried as hard as he could to keep up, but Normack was pulling ahead. The field they were so desperately racing through was littered with large boulders and crushed tree trunks with splintered tops. Slithering effortlessly back and forth and around every obstacle, Normack looked over with a grin on his face as Ty struggled to keep up. It seemed to take forever to cross that pasture, but they made it safely to the edge of the razor bushes in less than a minute.

"What are we going to do now, Normack?" Gasped Ty while

standing next to those bushes with his hands on his hips, trying to catch his breath.

"Just climb up on my back and hold on tight." He hissed while staring down at Ty. "I'll carry you over these weeds, but you can't tell anyone I did this, ever. If anyone found out that you rode me like a horse, I'll never live it down."

"Thank you. Thank you very much. I won't forget it, and I swear I'll never tell anyone. Now let's get this over with."

Ty didn't wait another second. He leaped up on Normack's hard scaly back, then grabbed ahold of one of his scales as tight as he could. Normack turned and glanced back at Ty to make sure he was ready. Then with one smooth slithery motion, they gently rose and started to glide over those dangerous bushes. You could hear the sharp leaves scratching and slicing against Normack's thick scales as they brushed against that thick row of bushes just inches below Ty's feet.

As soon as they made it safely to the other side, Ty slid off and started jumping around. "Wow, that was so cool! Just like a roller-coaster ride in a carnival. I've got to try that again! But next time, I want some cotton candy."

"Very funny fish feet, but you must keep your voice down. Grog's territory is right up ahead, and it goes all the way to the edge of the blue fields, and that's still far away. He could be anywhere."

Ty's little moment of fun was over; his smile and laughter faded away. He realized they were close to Grog's home turf's edge, and the Crystal Mountain was still so far away. Ty nodded his head silently and didn't say another word. After a few minutes, they made it out of that patch of woods and were standing next to a barren wasteland pounded flat with only a handful of shattered rocks and boulders scattered around. There were no more shadows to sneak around in or any trees to hide behind. But off in the distance, they could see the blue fields swaying in the soft sunlight beyond that barren wasteland, and Ty wasn't going to let anything stop him now.

"Hey, Normack, the coast looks clear to me. Let's go for it." Whispered Ty as he stood up and gave him a nudge in his side. "All we've gotta do is head straight over the next hill and we're home free."

"Don't be so sure, little one. We're not home free yet." He hissed in a soft, calm voice. "It's still a long way to the blue fields."

"I know that," whispered Ty as he stuck his spear in the ground. "But I don't want to hang around here anymore, so come on."

They both took a deep breath to regain their confidence and headed across the open field. After twenty minutes, Ty climbed over a large, smooth boulder in the middle of the field, stopped right in his tracks, and gazed up ahead.

"Look, there it is Normack!" Ty boasted out loudly as he stood there so proud. "There's the Crystal Mountain just over the next hill. It's more beautiful than anything I've ever seen!" Ty was jumping up and down, bursting with excitement. "Check it out, Normack. When the sun hits it, it looks like a rainbow glowing on the ground. It must be one gigantic cluster of crystals."

"Would you be quiet?" snapped Normack as he slid closer to Ty. "If you ever want to see it up close, you have to stay quiet!"

"Ok, ok. I didn't mean to yell like that. You're right. Let's get going."

Just as they started to climb down that boulder, the ground started to shake and rumble.

"Watch out, Normack! It's an earthquake!"

"I don't think it's an earthquake. I think we're in big trouble!"

Ty tried his best to keep his balance as the boulders rocked and rumbled under his feet. The hill was trembling so hard they had to dive for safety on the dusty ground below.

"You've got to be kidding me!" Ty shouted as he watched the hill starting to move and sway. "This is not good! Let me guess, Normack. That's Grog."

"You're pretty smart for a loudmouth fool," shouted Normack as he coiled up, ready for a fight. "What gave it away?"

They frantically looked around for somewhere to hide, but there wasn't anything around. Then slowly rising up from the deep pile of rubble came a creature made of solid rock. Its legs were wide and strong, and its body looked like someone had chiseled massive muscles on the side of a mountain. As Ty stood there with his mouth hanging open, he just couldn't believe how huge it was. Even though Ty was standing on the lip of a huge black boulder, he barely came up to its waist.

Then with a low grumbling roar, it stretched its gigantic arms in the air as its muscles started to ripple in the bright sunlight.

"Pssst, Normack, what should we do?"

"Shhhh. Whatever you do, just don't make it mad!" whispered Normack as he started to slither away slowly.

Ty shrugged his shoulders, trying to figure out what he shouldn't do as they stood there face-to-face. Suddenly a shiver ran through Ty's soul as the sound of its powerful stone muscles began grinding together when it turned its head and looked down on our two friends with its two bloodred eyes.

For a moment, Ty was frozen with fear, but after looking back at Normack, he knew he had to do something. "Hey, Grog, I really hope you don't mind us cutting through your yard. We're just passing by on our way to that field over there. So you can just lie back down and go back to sleep. I swear we won't bother you at all."

Grog stared down at Ty and Normack and started to tremble. But as Ty began to step away from that frightening mountain of stone, it arched its back and raised its enormous fists in the air. Then letting out a mighty roar, it slammed its fists into the ground. A thunderous blast rumbled across the land as a cloud of dust rose up and swirled around their legs.

"Guess not," muttered Ty as he took a big gulp and looked back at Normack again.

"Run!" Shouted Normack as his bright green eyes grew huge with fear, "run for your life! I'll try to hold it down so you can escape!"

Normack struck as fast as lightning, wrapping all around Grog, then squeezing it with all his might. "Run! Run now and getaway!"

"I won't leave you!" screamed Ty as he drew his bow and

fired an arrow right into Grog's neck!

Smack, the arrow hit its mark with a mighty crack then shattered into a hundred pieces. But Grog never even flinched as he grabbed Normack behind his head and started to pounding him to death.

"Run, Ty! Please! I can't hold him much longer!" begged Normack as he started losing his grip. "Get out of here now."

Boom! Boom! Boom! Grog's brutal punches sent shock waves rippling through Normack's body as he desperately tried to pin his arm down. Blow after blow, Ty watched helplessly as Normack slowly started to slide off Grog as his grip faded away. His vicious attack was taking its toll. Normack was being beaten badly.

Ty frantically looked around for something, anything he could use to get that rock monster off his friend. But there was nothing around, and Grog just continued to pound and pound on Normack.

"What are you waiting for? Save yourself!" grunted Normack softly as he slid to the ground. "Run to the blue fields! I can't hold him anymore. Just go!" he whispered as his tail began to twitch.

"I'm not leaving you!" shouted Ty as he threw another rock at Grog. "I've gotta plan."

Then readying another arrow, Ty drew back on his bow and shot Grog right in the face! The sound of that loud crack rippled across Grog's wasteland as the fragments from the arrow flew into its eyes.

Grog let out a cold and hateful roar so loud that it almost blew Ty to the ground.

"What's the matter? Didn't you like that arrow? Well, maybe you'll like this one better." boasted Ty as he drew back his bow once more and sent another arrow right between his eyes.

As the splintered pieces of his arrow fell to the ground, Ty leaped up on that huge black boulder and shouted out as loud as he could, "You better put my friend down right now, or I'm gonna cut you up into bricks and build an outhouse out of you!"

Grog's eyes glowed as red as fire as he roared out with the devil's rage. You could feel the electricity filling the air as

Grog's heart turned black with revenge. With one powerful move, Grog ripped Normack from around his feet and threw him across the clearing right into a tree stump.

Smash! Crack! A tremendous thud billowed across the land as big chunks ripped out of that tree trunk and shot off in every direction. Normack's head hit the ground with a hollow thump. His body twitched twice, then laid there motionless while a small trickle of blood oozed from his mouth just as his eyes slowly closed.

"You're gonna pay for that, boulder butt!" Ty screamed, and he fired another arrow right into Grog's chest. "Now come and get me, you jerk!"

Ty tucked his head down and bolted as fast as he could back into the forest with Grog right behind him, step for step. "Who knew this pile of rocks could move so fast?" Ty thought to himself as the ground started to crack apart with every pounding step it took.

Ty was sure he could outrun it, but Grog was way too fast, and he wasn't slowing down at all. Ty darted between the trees and leaped over every small bush that stood in his way, heading straight for the row of razor bushes. He couldn't stop now, and there was nowhere else to go but straight into that razor-sharp death trap. As Ty came just inches away, he stuck his spear deep into the ground and hurdled over those bushes with one mighty leap!

With a solid thump, Ty stuck the landing on the other side, then spun around and screamed as loud as he could, "Next time, you better get those rocks out of your pockets if you are wanna catch me!"

Only Grog didn't stop at all. In fact, it didn't even slow down.

With nowhere to run, Ty stumbled backward a few steps then dove behind a tree just seconds before Grog went crashing into the razor bushes. Cowering down with his arms covering his head, Ty watched in shock as the razor bushes shattered like a wall of glass, sending jagged pieces flying in every direction and shredding everything it touched.

After a few seconds passed by, Ty peeked around that tree and saw Grog just standing there without a scratch. "I guess being made of stone has its privileges," muttered

Ty as he sprung to his feet and bolted away. "But it looks like you just can't take a hint, boulder boy. So if you wanna piece of me, just come and get it."

As Ty approached the forest, he really poured it on, weaving through the trees and leaping over the bushes as smoothly as a six-legged fire rasp. In fact, Ty was going so fast his legs were a blur. Soon, he could start to smell that awful stench again. So he sprinted over the last hill and headed straight for the slimy, gross swamp.

Grog pounded his fists furiously against his chest as he watched Ty starting to disappear into the woods. Then with one swipe of its huge hands, it ripped an old tree out of the ground and whipped it right at Ty's head. Its whooshing sound streamed through the forest as Ty looked over his shoulder and dove to the ground just as it came flying past like a cannonball.

"You throw like a two-year-old!" shouted Ty as he jumped over the last hilltop, disappearing past the mulberry bushes. "Come and get me if you got the rocks for it!"

Ty ran across the shore without ever looking back and jumped back onto what was left of the tree bridge as fast as he could. Then leaping from piece to piece, he made his way along the busted-up bridge. Then as soon as he made it about halfway, Ty ducked down as low as he could behind an old crooked branch covered with moss and held on as tight as he could, hoping Grog wouldn't be able to see him.

A few moments later, while he was crouched down low, Ty watched as Grog busted down the last few trees that stood in its way and came storming over the hill. Ty did everything he could to keep that log from rolling over as waves of muck and slime started to splatter against the tree from the shock waves of his thunderous steps.

With that busted old willow tree splashing back and forth, it only took a few seconds for Grog to spot Ty hanging on for his dear life. Ty was now totally trapped, and with the tree bridge rolling wildly in that bubbling goop, he couldn't do a thing to get away.

Grog let out a loud and vicious growl and came running across the shore and onto the bridge after Ty. But as Grog closed in, the tree bridge started snapping and popping under his tremendous weight.

Without warning, the tree bridge snapped like a twig, sending them both flying into that murky swamp head first. Grog began splashing wildly in that murky mess, flinging clumps of mud and grime in every direction. Despite everything it tried, there was no stopping it now. Grog was sinking fast, and in just moments, he was gone.

But Ty struggled desperately to keep his head out of the water as waves of muck came crashing down. But with all of Grog's smashing, there was nothing left of that tree to grab on to except a handful of bark and twigs. The more he splashed around, the harder it was for him to move. Ty was becoming exhausted, and the slime started to pull him down.

Slowly and quietly, the rushing waves of that black swamp grew still. The waters were quiet once more. Only the soft sound of gently rustling leaves came from the woods, and no sign of Ty anywhere. He was gone too.

Suddenly, a huge figure came bursting out from the bushes along the shore. It was Normack!

"What happened here? Ty, where are you? Ty! Ty!"

Normack scoured the shoreline, and the only footprints he could see led straight into the swamp. Normack slithered back and forth, flicking his tongue at every turn, trying to see any sign of where Ty could be. Just when Normack was about to give up, he spotted Ty's body bubbling up slowly from the bottom of that gloomy swamp, covered with black ooze. His green eyes grew huge as he witnessed that awful sight. Without hesitating for a second, Normack dove in after him. Swishing back and forth as fast as any vipercon has ever done before, he swam over, snatched him up, and got him to shore.

"Wake up, fish feet! I won't let you die after what you've done for me, so you better wake up right now!"

Ty's body lay there motionless on the cold and rocky ground. Normack yelled as loud as he could once more to wake him up, but it just didn't work. He knew Ty must have swallowed some of that black swamp water. So he coiled around Ty and gave him three strong squeezes until a large chunk of sludge shot out and splattered against Normack's chin. It took three more times before Ty slowly started to open his eyes and cough up more of that stinking black ooze.

"You better learn to swim if you're gonna try a stunt like that again," Normack smirked as he bent down, shaking his head. "We better get out of here before Grog returns."

"We won't have to worry about boulder butt anymore," Ty mumbled as he coughed and gagged on that slimy mess. "I took care of him real good."

"Why? What did you do?" snapped Normack as he looked back into the woods.

But Ty just sat up, pointing out toward the middle of the swamp. "Grog's somewhere out there, lying on the bottom of that puddle of puke! Since Grog's a rotten old rock monster, being trapped underwater shouldn't harm him at all. But that thing sure is in for a long walk if it ever wants to get out of that stink hole. Enough talk about pebble brains. I think I am going to get sick, and I need a bath, and I mean right now."

Then after staggering to his feet, Ty headed for the first clean puddle he saw and dove right in.

"What are you doing?" Normack chuckled while he watched Ty splashing around. "At least you don't smell like rotten fish feet anymore. I think it is an improvement!"

CHAPTER 4

AN UNEXPECTED SURPRISE

The way back to the great Crystal Mountain went by like a flash, especially since Grog had trampled down every tree and razor bush that stood in their way. (and believe me, that made a very nice road back) In no time at all, they were strolling through the blue fields headed to the base of that magnificent mountain. It looked even more beautiful up close, shining and glistening in the afternoon sun.

However, Normack started to complain that he was feeling exhausted and quite sore. That beating he got with Grog must have worn him out.

"I just need to rest for a little while," hissed Normack as he glided next to Ty. "I see a nice comfortable place in a clearing next to that tall silver tree, and it's got my name written all over it. So I'll see you in a little bit."

Ty just smiled and padded him on his back. "Go ahead and relax for a while and get some rest. You've earned it. I'm gonna take a look around. I'll be back in about an hour to check up on you, but if you need me, I'm going over to those caves next to that tall pillar over there."

Normack just peeked over to where Ty was pointing and let out a sigh. "No problem, fish feet. I'll see you in a while."

Ty just shook his head and smiled as he walked by Normack. But when he started to walk around him, he stepped in some sticky slime oozing out from under one of his scales.

"Yuck! What in the world is that? Hey, Normack, what's up with your scale over here? Is that normal?"

"My scales, what are you talking about? I'm fine. Just go ahead and check out those caves. I'll catch up with you later," snapped Normack as he nestled his head down in the sweet soft grass.

"I'm talking about this goop all over your side," he replied as he pointed at a puddle of nasty yellowy slime oozing from under one of Normack's scales.

"I don't know what you're talking about. The only thing wrong with me is that thanks to Grog, I have a pounding headache, and my side feels like it's been ripped in half from getting smashed against a tree."

"Hey, I'm not kidding here. I think you got an infection. My Mom always said if you have a cut and don't keep it clean, it'll get infected. So if you have a cut under your scale, that little swim in the swamp could cause a nasty infection. This looks serious, Normack. This goop dripping out over here stinks worse than that swamp did. Let me just check this out for you because there's something's not right."

"Whatever, just hurry up. I don't need anybody poking around me while I try to get some rest and warm my scales in the sun!"

"Don't worry about it. This shouldn't hurt a bit. All I have to do is to pry up on this scale a little to get a better look."

Ty reached down and tried to pull back on Normack's scale, but he couldn't get his fingers underneath it far enough to pull it back. So he stepped back and looked around for something he could use to help him get a better look. That's when he saw the perfect thing. He walked back and grabbed his spear, and used it to gently pry his scale up.

"That's perfect," snickered Ty after he tossed his spear down and shoved it up a bit harder with his hands. "Just relax and stay still for a minute while I check it out."

When he knelt on the ground and looked underneath that scale, Ty started to freak out. "Holy crap!" screamed Ty as he jumped back and grabbed his spear. "It's a life leech. You have a life leech stuck on you, Normack. That's why you're so tired and can't move. We have to get that thing off right now!"

"What in the world are you talking about?" huffed Normack when he rolled his head over at Ty.

"I said it's a life leech, you big dumb snake. They live on the blood and the life force of anything they can sink their teeth into, and the only thing that's left after a life leech is done feeding is a dried-up, hollow body!"

Normack looked over to where Ty was kneeling and started to chuckle. "You're crazy! No leech could ever bite through my scales no matter how tough they are."

"I never said it bit through your scales, you big idiot! It must've squirmed between them when you dove into the swamp to save me."

"That ridiculous." He hissed sharply back at Ty. "Look around you. Leeches crawl around on the ground, and I've never been attacked by one of your life leeches before!"

"Normack, I'm not kidding! Just listen. My Dad taught me all about these things. Life leeches can only survive in really dark places like that swamp because if they get caught in the sunlight for very long, their bodies dry out and get so hard it's like they turn into steel. That's why you've never saw one of them on the ground before. They can't survive in the woods."

"Well then, if you know so much about life leeches, what are you waiting for? Pull it off and step on it!"

"Normack, you don't understand! My Dad said that they can move as fast as lightning, and the only way you can kill one is to capture it in a net and leave it in the sun. But we don't have a net, and we don't have enough time to make one. I don't know what to do, Normack! I just don't know what to do!"

"Just take a deep breath," grumbled Normack as he laid his head down. "No leach can hurt me."

"I've gotta find something to use and fast, Normack!

Don't worry! I'll figure something out," shouted Ty as he started running around. But when he ran to the Crystal Mountain, hoping to find something he could use to defeat a life leech. There was absolutely nothing there, and Ty looked everywhere. Then as fast as he could, Ty ran back to Normack and told him, "I just won't give up on you. There's always something you can do."

Normack was getting weaker by the second, and he barely had enough strength left to keep his eyes open. Ty knew he was running out of time.

Ty ran back to the Crystal Mountain again and started digging around. He knew if he had a rope, he could tie it around that thing and rip it off. But there was nothing around he could use. Then turning around in pure frustration, Ty punched that crystal wall as hard as he could. Crack! The sound echoed across the blue fields like a firecracker. Ty grabbed his fist and screamed out in pain because it felt like he nearly broke every bone in his hand on that stupid rock. After stomping around, trying to get over the pain, he looked back at that spot where he smacked that rock and it nearly blinded him by the light shining off it.

"That's it! I've got it!" Ty screamed, jumping up and down. "This can work Buddy; I've got an idea. I just hope that I have enough time."

Moving as fast as he could, Ty ripped off his jacket and started rubbing and cleaning off all the dirt and grime from that crystal. He never stopped rubbing it until it sparkled like a mirror!

"Over here, Normack," yelled Ty as he pointed at the crystal like a mad man. "You've gotta come over here, right here. It's the only way to get that thing off you."

Normack struggled to open his eyes and looked over at Ty. "I don't think I can make it. I don't have enough strength left."

"You got to!" Ty screamed. "It's your only chance. Now get your scaly butt over here!"

Normack gathered all the strength he had left and slowly moved toward Ty.

"That's it, just a little further."

With the very last bit of energy that Normack could

muster, he made it to the spot that Ty was pointing to, then collapsed, exhausted. There was no more time left. This had to work, and it had to work right now! Ty grabbed his spear, wedged it deep under Normack's scale, and started prying it back as hard as he could. He pulled back that scale so far that he could see that huge leech feasting on what life Normack had left.

But he was scared that if he tried to stab it with his spear, he might miss and hurt Normack. So he held his spear like a baseball bat and whacked that life leech right on its back. Crack! He smacked that slimeball so hard his spear snapped in half. If that didn't get its attention, nothing would.

The moment Ty's spear snapped in half, that horrible creature let out a monstrous squeal that sounded like a vampire bat ripping into its prey. In a flash, it jerked its head out from under Normack's scale, and its six bright yellow eyes turned jet-black as it stared deep into Ty's eyes.

Ty jumped back as it let out another bone-chilling screech and opened up its blood-filled mouth. All he could see was row after row of razor-sharp green teeth, spinning around and around, still dripping with Normack's blood. Ty was never more scared in his life. He closed his eyes for a second and wished that his Dad was there with him, but he was all alone, staring right down the throat of that beast.

But he stood his ground and looked that thing right in its eyes. Then he opened his arms out wide, showing that beast his bare chest, and screamed as loud as he could, "If you want a piece of me, just come and get it!"

With a high-pitched shriek, it coiled up and prepared to attack. Quick as lightning, it shot out from under Normack's scale and headed straight for Ty's chest so fast he didn't have time to move!

Whack! It hit hard. The sickening sound of crushing flesh rippled across the blue field.

"Oh, man... it worked! I knocked it out cold." Ty boasted as he danced around in a circle. "That thing thought it was going to feast on me, but it was just my reflection on that crystal. When that slug tried to sink its teeth into my chest, all he got was a mouthful of rock! Did you hear me, Normack? I made that thing bite stone! It won't be feasting on anything anymore. I think it knocked all its teeth out too. You've gotta get up. We gotta get out of here fast. I don't want to be around when that thing wakes up."

Normack's eyes just fluttered open for a moment, then closed again. "You go, Ty. I'm just going to stay here and rest for a while. Don't worry about me. That thing's way too big now to fit under my scales. I'll be just fine."

"If you say so," Ty mumbled while checking over his shoulder back at that thing. "But if you don't mind, I need to see where it had ahold of you first."

Ty crept as carefully as he could around that life leech so he wouldn't wake it up, grabbed what was left of his spear, pried up that scale once again, and took a peek.

"Well, bud, it looks like you lost a lot of blood. The good news is the wound doesn't look too deep and the bleeding stopped. It's a good thing my Mom is a doctor. I know exactly what to do. They're plenty of healing plants growing all around these woods. I'll have you all fixed up in no time."

Ty ran over behind the silver tree and pulled up a handful of sponge moss that was growing on its roots and used it as a Band-Aid. But when Ty stepped over that life leech on his way to the forest again, he almost slipped in a pool of green blood by its head.

"Hey, wait a minute, that thing isn't knocked out. It's dead! Hey, Normack, it's dead. It's really dead!" screamed Ty as he jumped up and down. "I killed a life leach!"

Normack smiled and gave him a small nod. "I have to admit you sure are resourceful. Now if you don't mind, go away. I need to rest!"

But while Ty stood gloating over that dead life leech, he looked around and suddenly realized that he was almost out of weapons. His spear was broken, he only had two arrows left, and his knife was dull and chipped badly from slamming it into a tree. He knew he could fix his broken spear with a new staff and make some more arrows, except it still wouldn't be good enough if he ran across any really tough creatures like that rinog again.

So one more time, Ty was on the search for something he could use to make some weapons that would be strong enough to take him through his quest. He knew those crystals lying around were very strong, but they just weren't sharp enough to use.

But that's when Ty looked down at that disgusting life leech lying dead in the sun. He knew just what he had to do. Instead of letting that life leech go to waste, he figured he could use its hide to make everything he needed. Since Ty had ruined his jacket cleaning off that crystal, he took a moment to make himself a vest, then laid it out on top of the brightest crystal he could find so it could cure hard and strong. Next, he took a big piece, stretched it over a smooth curved boulder, and formed it into a perfect shield. Ty started to grin as he smoothed it out and trimmed off its ragged edges. He knew right away that if he could get it to cure properly, it would stand up to anything that place could ever dish out.

The one thing he needed more than anything else was a weapon that could stand up to anything that lurked in the Shadow Forest. So Ty took his time and polished a golden crystal as smooth and bright as he could, then laid a piece as long as his arm gently on top of it. He took great care in shaping it into the perfect sword, then used the fang he took from Normack to form a mighty hilt. He knew right away that a sword created from the hide of a life leech would be strong enough to fight a bear.

When he was finally sure that he was done, he placed another golden crystal on top to keep it perfectly flat and in perfect shape while it dried. However, when Ty placed those two crystals together, a blinding golden light shot out from between them like *a starburst and knocked him to the ground.

"This is going to be awesome," he thought to himself as he stood back up, giggling with joy.

Finally, he took what was left and cut it into one long strip, and stretched it as tight as he could between two large trees. With his time starting to run out before it turned to steel, he ran around and flipped over every flat rock he could see, hoping to find some oily stipple moss. After about ten minutes, he was about to give up until he flipped over a long crystal shard at the edge of the forest and found a nice thick batch of that oily, sludgy mess.

38 An Unexpected Surprise

"This might work," he said softly to himself because he knew that if there was anything that could stop a life leech skin from turning hard, it had been that slimy sludge. So he scooped up a nice, big, dripping handful, ran back, and smeared it all over that strip so it would slowly soak in and keep it from drying out too fast.

"What are you doing over there?" whispered Normack while he watched Ty running back and forth.

"Well, I'm trying to make a rope. But if that stipple moss doesn't work, I guess I just made one really long and slippery pole." He chuckled as he wiped his hands off in the dirt.

For once, Ty figured he had everything he needed to survive this terrible place, or at least he would finally have a fighting chance.

So he spun around with his arms folded in front of him and looked over at Normack, and began tapping his foot like his Mom always did. "What you need is some food to help you build up your strength and some medicine to help your injuries heal. Since my sword is drying, I'll just take my bow and go hunting to get you something to eat. Now you save your strength and warm yourself in the sun, and I'll be back soon."

Normack nodded his head and closed his eyes. He never put that much trust in anyone else, but he knew that he could trust Ty with his life after what just happened.

CHAPTER 5

ALONE AGAIN
IN THE SHADOW FOREST

After his triumphant battle against a full-grown life leach, he had the confidence to go out alone. So he grabbed his knife and bow and then headed for the forest. He wasn't sure what he could get for Normack to eat, but the forest was big, and he wouldn't go back without something. Unfortunately, Ty knew that this could turn out to be a bigger challenge than he would admit. The only hunting he's ever done was for frogs and turtles, back at the river at home. So having a fifty-foot vipercon to feed was way over his head.

As he strolled across the blue field, he started to think about all the adventures he had been through. Ty would never have imagined his trip into the Shadow Forest would've turned out like it had. Before long, He was back in the shade of that creepy forest again, except this time, instead of running from the beasts that live in the forest, he was looking to take one down.

Walking through the trees and moving as silently as a Ghost, his senses felt sharp and crisp. The sweet scent of freshly fallen leaves and the sound of the trees swaying in the slight breeze was like soft music that fills the air in a dream.

The further he went, he began noticing all the different animal tracks around him. Some he could recognize, like those of a small rabbit and a deer, but the tracks he found next to a boulder made him quite nervous. Those tracks definitely belonged to a huge red-tailed wolf. The wolf tracks, thank goodness, seemed to be a couple of days old, but the deer tracks he spotted were fresh.

"Finally, some good luck for a change," Ty thought to himself while kneeling down and running his fingers across those tracks. "Bringing back a deer for Normack would get his strength back quick. But if I run into a wolf out here, I'm gonna be in big trouble."

Ty picked up a few leaves and let them drift out of his hands. Watching closely as they floated to the ground, thinking, "Perfect, the wind is blowing towards me and that means nothing out here in this creepy place will get a whiff of my scent until it's too late." So he started to follow those deer tracks through the forest, staying in the shadows and moving as quietly as he could. They led him through fields of thick brush and over steep hills until finally, they led into a small valley full of rich berry bushes and lush green trees.

His eyes filled with excitement as he looked all around. Ty knew that deer had to be close. Staying hidden behind a tree, he studied the area ahead, paying close attention to every place a deer could be hiding behind. He was hoping to spot any sign where it went like bent twigs, folded-over grass, or maybe even a bird suddenly springing up and flying away. The more he watched, the more disappointed he got. Even the tracks he was following seemed to disappear into the soft grass ahead.

"Just another dead end," Ty thought to himself while a nest of birds chirped softly high in the tree above him. But just as he was going to give up, he heard some leaves softly rustling up ahead. The hairs on the back of his neck started to tingle. That wasn't the sound of leaves swirling in the wind. There was something else there, something big.

Up ahead, on the far side of the clearing, he watched as three small twigs slowly bend over then snap back into the air. With a grin on his face, Ty got down on his belly and crawled closer to a berry bush. Suddenly, the sound of a small twig snapping rang out beneath him. He froze for a second, then rolled behind a large tree, and held his breath. He peeked around the tree and saw the bushes rustle again; there was definitely something in there.

Ty sat there quietly, watching and squinting his eyes as hard as he could to make out what was lurking behind those bushes. That's when he started to piece together the different patterns of tracks he was following. The deer tracks seemed deep and gashed across the ground, while the wolf tracks were soft and crossed the deer's path in a zigzag pattern. He realized he wasn't the only thing hunting that deer. That wolf must be around here somewhere, and if it couldn't take down that deer, then it just might try to hunt him instead.

So Ty took a deep breath and watched silently as the bushes slowly swayed to the side as if something large started pushing against it. You could hear the faint sound of cautious steps walking across the soft grass, like a predator on the prowl. Whatever it was behind that brush, it was starting to come out. Then Ty reached for his bow, slid an arrow between his fingers, and held his breath as a large shadow drifted between the twigs, headed for the clearing.

There it was, the biggest deer he had ever seen. Its soft brown coat blended perfectly with the woods behind it while its large rack of antlers seemed to hold its head still. "What a perfect shot," Ty thought to himself as he watched it ease into the field. It had no idea Ty was there as it bowed its head to nibble the grass. Suddenly, the deer twitched and stood up straight. You could see its huge muscles rippling as it nervously stared into the forest. Ty held his breath and stayed perfectly still, hoping the deer wouldn't see him. It seemed like time slowed down, and every second crawled by as that deer scanned for danger.

"Wow, it looks so cool," thought Ty. It looked so strong and fearless, standing there firmly with the sun glistening off its antlers. But he knew what he had to do, so he slowly drew back his bowstring and held his breath to steady his aim. He gazed deeply into those dark brown eyes as he drifted his aim to its heart.

"I just can't do it," Ty whispered in frustration.

Ty closed his eyes and slowly exhaled. A sense of calm ran through his body like a warm wave as he lowered his bow and slung it back over his shoulder. He watched for a few more minutes in amazement as it flinched once more and started to graze again. Ty thought about Normack and the promise he made. But he just couldn't bring himself to do it. So Ty slowly took a step out from behind that tree to see that remarkable animal better.

In an instant, the deer's head snapped back and quickly spotted Ty standing there. Hesitating just for a moment, as if to say thank you, it raised its front hoofs up and bolted for the safety of the forest. Ty just stood there leaning against the tree and watched as the tall grass swayed back and forth as it disappeared into the forest.

"There's no way I could have dragged it back anyway," Ty muttered as he started to head back to the crystal mountain, upset with himself that he didn't kill the deer. But deep down inside, he knew he had done the right thing. He figured it wouldn't be a total loss because he remembered while he was tracking the deer, he had passed some aloe plants that he could use for Normack's wounds and a strong willow tree with some real old bark that he could use to make some medicine to ease his friend's pain.

Ty knew the aloe plants were going to be easy to get. They were growing right next to the trail he was following, so on his way back, he just broke off a handful of leaves and stuffed them into his pocket.

The next thing on his list was the willow bark, which was going to be a bit harder to get because the willow tree was on the other side of a creek. It might not seem like such a big deal, but the sides of the creek were steep and muddy. Ty knew that if he wasn't careful, he could fall into the fast-moving water below and drown. So he took his time, walked downstream a bit, and found a safer place to cross. In no time at all, he was standing on the other side and making his way back to the willow tree.

Considering how big Normack was, Ty knew he needed the most potent medicine bark he could get his hands on. That meant he needed to get some off the very top branches. So when Ty got back to that great willow tree and stood there for a minute, looking it over very carefully. Then with a big, excited grin, he grabbed the closest branch and swung into action. He pulled himself up with one quick tug then pounced from limb to limb, getting higher and higher.

Ty was having fun again as he raced to the very top of that tree, but his fun seemed to end in a flash as he flipped over the last twisted limb and reached the top of that huge tree. He sat down on that last crooked limb, pulled out his knife, and went to work stripping big handfuls of fresh bark from the most potent parts of the branch. Within minutes, he had everything he needed, and his pouch was stuffed to the top.

While sitting high in the tree and swinging his feet back and forth, Ty could see the top of the Crystal Mountain glittering in the sun. The magnificent colors streaming off it made his heart start pounding as the excitement rushed through his veins. "There had to be huge blue fire rubies scattered all over that mountain," he thought while the anticipation started to boil inside him.

Eager to get going, he started swinging and jumping from branch to branch, making his way back down. When Ty made it to the bottom branch, he dove off it like a springboard and hit the ground so hard his legs sank into the sandy forest floor right up to his knees. Ty took one look at his legs as he tried to wiggle them out and then burst out laughing. "Now that's how you stick a landing!"

After Ty had a good laugh, he tried to get out, but he couldn't move an inch. He was completely stuck. All he needed was some good leverage to get him out, and the only thing close enough for him to grab was one of the tree's thick roots.

"That'll work," Ty thought to himself as he leaned out for the root, but as he stretched across the ground, he heard a loud snap. "That don't sound good," he mumbled to himself as he looked around at the ground. Then another pop rang out and the ground started to shake. Ty looked around and held on tight. "This is definitely not going to be good."

In a flash, the ground started to crumble and collapse as Ty kept struggling to drag himself free. Another chunk of dirt gave way and disappeared into a crack in the ground that began to grow larger right next to his legs. Then suddenly, another snap rang out, and Ty sank up to his chest. He knew he had to get out of this mess fast, so he stretched out as far as he could and had just barely gotten a few fingers around that old tree root when the rest of the ground fell away.

"Oh crap!" shouted Ty as he hung on to that root with all his might as dirt and rocks disappeared into a deep crevice below.

After a few seconds had passed, the ground stopped shaking and Ty was still hanging there, swinging back and forth on that slippery old root. Then with a smirk on his face, he shook off a clump of mud stuck to his back and shouted down that deep, dark hole, "You'll have to do better than that to get me!" Then reaching up with his other hand, he grabbed that old root as it snapped in half, sending him tumbling down the hole.

Bouncing and crashed into its rocky walls, he fell helplessly into the darkness with a chunk of that root still locked in his grip. A hollow thud echoed through the cave when Ty slammed to the ground as a vail of dirt sprinkled down and covered the floor.

As he laid there sprawled out across the ground, the cave seemed to come alive with bats zipping around in circles and centipedes roaming across the ground.

"Dang that hurt," mumbled Ty while rubbing his head and spitting out pieces of dirt. "Now what am I going to do?"

Ty just plopped his head back down and closed his eyes, trying to get the ringing in his ears to stop. While he was thinking about what he was going to do next, he was completely unaware of the huge, hairy spiders, the size of your fist, scurrying out of the shadows in every direction.

Like an arrow flying to its target, they zipped across the floor and jumped all over Ty, spinning their webs as fast as they could. It only took them a few seconds to cast a silky blanket, covering his arms and legs and pinning him to the ground. But as they began to crawl over his chest, their hairy legs started to tickle and scratch. Ty's eyes sprung open just as one started to cast its web across his face.

"What the heck's going on?" screamed Ty as he stared right in the face of one of those nasty things.

"Get off me, you eight-legged creep!" screamed Ty again as he tried to knock it off, but no matter how hard he tried, he couldn't even move. The spiderwebs were too strong. All he could manage to do was stretch them out just a few inches.

But the more he struggled the madder he got. Until he got so mad, he started gritting his teeth, and he yanked his arm free and pulled out his knife.

"Now you're in trouble!" roared Ty as he flicked one of those hairy spiders off of his neck.

Then working as fast as he could, he started slashing and slicing his way through that web of death. But when Ty finally freed himself, he jumped up and started kicking those spiders across the cavern and stomping the rest of them into the ground. For the next few minutes, he just stood there shaking mad and peeling that sticky web off and flicking it to the ground.

"I hate this place!" he bellowed loud and strong after stomping on the last spider as it tried to scurry away.

He knew the worst thing he could do was panic, so after taking a moment to calm down, he tried climbing back up that pit. But the walls were so loose and crumbly, every time he tried to climb up, big chunks of dirt and rocks peeled away and came crashing down. He had to find another way out.

After giving up trying to climb out of there, he finally looked around that damp and musty cave and saw a little flicker of light squeezing out from the darkness and mumbled to himself, "Cool, there's some daylight up ahead. This shouldn't be too hard."

Ty took a deep breath and started to feel his way through that dark and creepy cavern. He was having a real hard time finding his way through the darkness. No matter how hard he tried, he kept tripping over the crooked roots and all those loose rocks scattered across the ground. But at least it became easier the closer he got to that light. Just as Ty walked around the last corner, he stopped right in his tracks and smiled.

He found himself standing in the opening of an even larger cave with vast deposits of star crystals sticking out of the walls. Ty never saw so many star crystals in one place before in his whole life; the entire cave was shining as bright as day!

"All right!" Ty yelled out as loud as he could. "Nothing can stop me now!"

While his voice was still echoing off the walls, he knew his search for the blue fire rubies just got a whole lot easier. With a huge smile on his face, he ran right up to the biggest one he could reach and ripped it down. The bright white light that shot out of that crystal nearly blinded him as he stood there checking it out.

Instantly, he knew that he would never again have a problem making his way through any of those deep, dark caves ever again. So he quickly put that star crystal to good use and started sprinting through the cavern as fast as his legs could go. "This is so cool," Ty thought as its light danced across the walls. "I can't wait to show Normack what I've found."

With his feet digging deep into the soft dusty ground, he bolted through the winding cave like a fire rasp through a field. Then after a few short minutes, he started grinning from ear to ear again when he saw the sweet green trees of the Shadow Forest up ahead. But as he approached the opening of the cave, he slowed down and started walking out boldly with his head held high and with new confidence that nothing was going to stop him now. Then just as he cleared the entrance of that cave, he spotted something out of the corner of his eye. It was moving around behind the bushes right next to the entrance. So he took his time to lay his bow gently on the ground and knelt down to get a better look.

"Wow, would you look at that," he muttered softly as a smile swept across his face.

Then taking great care not to make a sound, he slowly

snuck around the side of that bush. When Ty was inches away, he silently pulled out his knife and dove right in. The bushes shook wildly as Ty rolled through the brush, kicking and swinging away. In just a few moments, those bushes stopped shaking, and the sounds of a life and death struggle slowly faded away.

Covered with scratches and giggling with excitement, he stood up proudly with a smile on his face. He was holding his prize, still wiggling and scratching as it tried to get away. It was a big white chicken, clucking and flapping its wings violently and making a big racket, but there was no way Ty was going to let this one get away.

"Well, it's not as big as a deer," Ty thought to himself while shrugging his shoulders. "But Mom always says there's nothing better than chicken soup to help you feel better." So, Ty put his knife away and grabbed his bow and proudly started back to the Crystal Mountain with that chicken held tightly in his grip.

It felt like he was gone for hours, but when Ty finally made it back to the blue fields, he could see Normack still asleep in the warm summer sun.

"Hey Normack, wake up," yelled Ty as he held that bird as high as he could. "I bought you something to eat and got some medicine too."

As Ty causally strolled across that field and got about halfway through, he started to notice the sounds of the soft tall grass crunching delicately behind him. But when he spun around to see what it was, he couldn't see a thing. That's when he noticed the crickets chirping in the weeds had already gone silent. He knew deep in his bones, he was in big trouble as those soft crunching sounds turned into a hard and deep thumping, getting closer and closer.

So he took off running as fast as his legs could carry him, but when he looked over his shoulder, the only thing he saw was the tall grass flying in the air and cutting a path straight for him. Ty dropped that chicken and poured on all the speed he had left, but in a split second, it felt like someone clobbered him in the back with a sledgehammer, sending him tumbling across the ground.

That was when Ty finally saw what was after him. His eyes

filled with horror as he watched a five-foot-tall vicious cave rat slowly circling around him with its head shaking back and forth. Its long, oily black hair and razor-sharp yellow teeth stained with the blood of its last victim. He knew right away that it must have followed him from those caverns because cave rats rarely come out in light of day.

Ty rolled over on his back and started kicking and struggling as hard as he could, trying to keep it away long enough so he could escape. After it circled him one more time, it crouched down low then pounced. "Holy crap," he shouted as he kicked it hard in the head and sent it tumbling backward into the grass with a loud smack.

Seeing his chance to escape, Ty spun around and tried to get up as it pounced again, pinning him flat on the ground. "Get off me!" Ty screamed as he reached up and grabbed that thing by its throat, trying desperately to stop it from sinking its teeth deep into his chest. He fought back with every ounce of energy he had as it snapped and chomped wildly just inches from his face.

While it ferociously kept scratching and pawing across his stomach, Ty managed to snatch his knife from his side and jabbed it into its mouth deep and hard. But the beast just shook its head and snapped his stone knife in half with an eerie pop.

Ty started screaming as loud as he could and grabbed it by its throat to shove it straight back again. But Ty wasn't strong enough to throw it very far. It was way too big. As it flew back onto its hind legs, it shook its head wildly and pounced again.

The fields flooded with its high-pitched screech when it landed right on Ty's chest and used its paws to pin both of his hands right to the ground. Ty struggled as hard as he could to get up, but he couldn't move at all. He was trapped. Ty looked up into those beady black eyes and watched helplessly as it opened its up mouth wide. He could see bits of flesh that was still stuck in its teeth, and he could smell the nasty stench of rotting flesh oozing out from its mouth. That's when he heard a sound that would send a ghost screaming in the dark—the crunch of teeth slicing through bone.

Ty was in shock, frozen solid on the ground. He couldn't believe his eyes as he watched Normack sink his fangs deep into that filthy rat's chest. Twisting and spinning savagely, Normack had it trapped in his coils in a blink of an eye.

When Normack had it firmly twisted in his grasp, he looked down at Ty and tried to give him a little smile with the rat still wedged in his jaws, "How did you know there's nothing better than a cave rat to help you feel better?" He hissed sarcastically while giving him a nudge. "Next time, if I were you, I wouldn't get so close to them. They do have a nasty bite if you're not careful."

"Oh, that's disgusting," Ty said as he watched its tail slide down Normack throat. "By the way, Normack, how did you do that with one fang missing?"

"What do you mean? I have all four of my fangs." He snapped back with a grin. "Sometimes a vipercon can lose a fang when we strike or when a small meal rips one out! So they grow back quickly,"

Ty looked at Normack and laughed. "After you're done eating that rat, I want to put this medicine on you to help you heal. In the meantime, I guess I'll have some chicken for lunch. That is if I can find it again."

"You're going to eat a bird? Now that's gross."

Ty just laughed a little and shook his head. He knew that Normack just saved his life, and he was still shaken up a bit. "If you don't mind, I'll meet you back at the mountain. I've got a chicken to catch. Again!"

CHAPTER 6
WEAPONS ARE FORGED

It didn't take Ty long at all to track down that bird. He found it stuck under a thistle bush, trying to hide. But this time, he didn't have to dive in after it. All he had to do was reach in and pull it out by its feet.

"You made that look easy." Snickered Normack while he waited by his side. "You must have a stronger stomach than I do. There's a reason we call them fowl."

On their way back to the Crystal Mountain, Ty picked up some dry twigs and sticks to make a fire so he could cook his lunch. At the speed they were going, it didn't take them long until they were back. As soon as they arrived Normack coiled up and laid his head back down in the soft silky grass. But Ty was too busy to sit back and enjoy the nice summer sun. The first thing he did was make a big fire next to the crystal pillars and surrounded it with pieces of shattered stones to keep it from getting out of control, just like his dad did when they went camping.

While Ty's food was cooking, he reached into his bag, pulled out the willow bark, and started to grind it into powder between two pieces of crystals. He picked out all the black flakes that would make the medicine bitter and gritty. When he had made a pile of soft white powder large enough to fill the palm of his hand, he smiled brightly because he knew he had made the medicine right, and it looked like it was going to be perfect to help Normack.

"Hey, Normack, this is like aspirin. It's a powerful medicine that will ease the pain from that battle you had with Grog. I learned how to make it from watching my Mom. All you have to do is swallow it, and you'll start feeling a lot better real quick." So Ty wrapped it up in some leaves so Normack didn't have to taste it and dropped it on Normack tongue.

"Thank you, Ty. I didn't know your Mom was a witch."

"She's not a witch. She's a doctor. She helps the people at home when they get hurt or need medicine. Now I picked up some more stuff here that will help that wound under your scale heal quicker. So I have to take a look under that scale again."

"Whatever you say, little doctor," Normack hissed gently as he slithered over to Ty.

Then laying his head down in the cool grass, he tried very hard to relax his scales so they would be easier to pull back. When Ty pried up the scale still stained with a little bit of slime, he was amazed at how well it was healing.

"Normack, this doesn't look as bad as I thought it would. But I'll still spread some aloe on it to make sure that you won't get an infection."

He split the aloe leaf open, scraped out the gel, and put it under Normack's scale. Then he used a little that was left over to smear on his own scrapes that he got tumbling down that hole and fighting that cave rat.

"Normack, there's one more thing you could use, and I think it might be the most important thing I can do for you." Snickered Ty kind of sarcastically, then he walked over to the silver tree that Normack was lying under when they first got to the Crystal Mountain and picked a few leaves from a small plant growing between its roots.

"Now, Normack, you have to chew these up good and swish it around your mouth before you swallow it. Okay?"

Normack agreed and did just what he was told. "This taste pretty good," Normack admitted as a smile drifted across his face. "What is this medicine going to do?"

"That's the one thing you needed the most. They're called mint leaves, and they can wipe out the worst case of rat breath that you can come up with."

"What did you say?" shouted Normack as he rose up and snapped his tongue. "You tricked me. Tell me, little man-child. If that works so well on my breath, then why don't you use a handful on those fish feet of yours?"

Ty started to laugh really hard and then grabbed a big handful of mint leaves. "I don't know if it will, but let's find out, Normack." Ty giggled some more as he started rubbing them all over his feet.

After a few more minutes of well-earned fun, Ty slipped his shoes back on and noticed his meal was finally done to a wonderful golden brown. He pulled it off the fire and offered some to Normack, but he just shook his head and turned his nose up and told him the rat he had was enough.

While Ty sat back and started enjoying his meal, he began to think about how close he had come to being eaten alive, and all the laughter faded away. Things didn't seem to be very funny anymore. When Ty finished his meal, he looked over at the armor he had made and knew it was time to get serious and get what he came for. He kicked some sand on the fire and stirred the coals to make sure it was smothered. Then he walked over, picked up the armor, and was shocked that it was as light as a feather. Ty sure hoped that it would fit because it wouldn't bend or flex no matter how hard he tried. It took a while to squeeze into that armor, but it fit him better than he could have ever hoped for.

Next, he grabbed his shield, but it felt like it was made of cardboard. "Boy, this doesn't seem like it's going to be strong enough to stop an attack from a butterfly," Ty thought while swung it around in the air. But he was smart enough to know he had to test it out before he had to use it in battle. So he looked around for something to test it on. Not far from the silver tree, he found a crystal as hard as a diamond growing out of the mountainside. This was going to be a perfect test. Ty walked over to that shard, then reached back and smacked the shield on that crystal with all his might. Boom! That smack rumbled across the field like a sledgehammer. Ty stood there with his mouth wide open; he couldn't believe his eyes. The crystal shattered into a million pieces.

"Hey, Normack, that crystal just shattered like glass, and I didn't even feel a thing." As Ty took a real good look at that shield where he hit that crystal, he couldn't believe it. There wasn't a single scratch on it. His armor and shield turned out ten times stronger than anything he could have possibly hoped for.

After Ty clipped his shield on his side, he headed over to where he had that leech skin smeared with moss, hopping his trick worked so he could still use it for a rope. When he got there, he was amazed it was still flexible and as strong as steel. Ty had done a great job making sure it didn't cure too fast and keeping it from turning into a long steel pole. With a grin on his face, he grabbed a handful of grass and whipped off the slippery oil, and quickly rolled up the rope and slung it over his shoulder.

Then with a deep breath, the time had finally come to claim his sword. Ty was kind of nervous as he made his way back to where it was hidden. As he walked around the backside of the mountain, he saw that the golden light was still sparking and shooting out from between those two crystals, except it was twice as intense as before. With each step he took, his heart started pounding faster and faster as the soft humming sound of racing electricity started to emanate from between those crystals.

Ty stood in the glow of the light, nervous and excited. He slowly reached out and lightly felt the top crystal, then pulled his hand back quickly in surprise. The crystal was as cold as ice around the edges but hot as dragon's breath across the top. He took another deep breath, gathered his nerve, reached down, picked up a few thick leaves, and used them to protect his hands. Then straining with all his might, he slowly lifted that heavy crystal from atop his sword and threw it to the ground. A burst of light shot out across the field like lightning and lit up the Shadow Forest for miles.

That was when he first saw his incredible sword. Its once leathery blade turned silvery grey and sparkled with the power of the golden light. At the same time, its curved ivory vipercon fang hilt was covered with a thick layer of icy frost. Ty stood there for a few minutes, watching as the beautiful light flickered like fire across the crystal, then he took another deep breath and reached out to pick it up. The moment he touched its hilt, the humming stopped, and the golden light flickered and went out with a flash.

As he lifted his sword, small sparks shot out from the crystal and raced up his arm and through his body. It was as if the magical power of the Crystal Mountain was unleashed into that sword.

Ty looked behind him at the mountain, then across the field to the edge of the Shadow Forest. That uneasy feeling in the pit of his stomach went away in the blink of an eye. He no longer feared cave rats, giant wolves, or any other creature that roamed in the shadows. For the first time since he came to that forest, he felt truly safe and in control of everything around him. At that moment, Ty stopped being a boy and saw the world through the eyes of a man.

Standing tall, with his sword held high, Ty shouted boldly into the sky, "I came here into these woods on a quest, and no creature, great or small, can stop me. So hear these words and be warned because if you try, you'll be defeated!"

Just then, Normack came rushing around the corner, wondering what all the commotion was about. When he saw Ty standing there with his armor shining in the sun and his sword held high, his green eyes opened wide, and he froze solid in disbelief.

"Is that you, fish feet?" Normack hissed, his voice stuttered with wonderment. "It sounded like someone was over hers, boasting like an idiot."

Ty spun around and put his sword away. "Yeah, of course it's me. What in the world's wrong with you Normack? It looks like you have seen a ghost or something!"

"I'm okay," stammered Normack as he slid around Ty's side. "You just look so different, and the way you're standing there reminds me of a story about a mighty warrior."

Normack started to tell Ty the story about a mighty warrior that battled many creatures, and when he came out of the Shadow Forest, he flew across the sky like an eagle to battle against the mightiest creature of all.

Ty smiled and nodded his head. "I know all about that story too. My history teacher told us all about it. Ms. Sue said his name was Cobasfang."

Ty looked down at his armor and then at Normack and busted out laughing, "You thought I was Cobasfang? That's the craziest thing I've ever heard. I'm only a boy, not to mention that I don't have any wings, and I can't fly."

"I know you're not Cobasfang, but the way you were standing there with the light shining on that sword just made me think of the story, that's all. Anyway, there's no way a warrior as great as Cobasfang could ever walk around in these woods with feet that smell as bad as yours do."

Ty looked up at Normack and started laughing again. "Well, Normack, I hope you're done making fun of my feet because I'm dying to get inside some of these caves and find some blue fire rubies."

"I'm not done making fun of you yet, little man-child. But if you're ready, I'll stop for a while and help you look in those caves too."

Ty had a little smirk on his face because he had a smart-aleck comment he was going to say, but he was so anxious to start looking he could hardly control himself. There were so many caves to explore; he didn't know where to start. So they decided to split up to cover more ground.

Boiling with excitement, Ty reached into his pocket, pulled out his star crystal, and ran into the nearest cave he could find. He zipped through it in no time at all, but the only thing he found inside were a few hairy spiders clinging to the walls. So he bolted out of that cave and into another as quickly as he could. Then another and another. It seemed like they were bouncing from one cave to another all day long, and the only thing they found were bats, rats, and some nasty hairy spiders.

Ty figured that he might have better luck if he could find a really deep cave that leads far below the Crystal Mountain, so he headed out to find the darkest corner on the farthest side. He searched everywhere for a way in, but the walls were too thick to break through and so smooth he couldn't climb up and look for an entrance above.

Ty was determined to find a way inside. But just as he was about to head back to find Normack, he walked past a clump of bushes and felt a cold breeze drifting through its branches.

"This has got to be the place," muttered Ty as he waved his hands around the bushes, feeling the cool soft draft. "There must be a hidden cavern somewhere around here."

So, he didn't waste another moment and pulled out his sword and began slashing his way through its thick, stout branches. His heart pounded with excitement; he could feel the cool cave air rushing over him as he slashed his way deeper into the brush. Once he sliced past the last clump of branches, he saw a wide split in the crystal wall.

"This is so awesome!" Ty shouted as he peered into the crack. "Hey Normack, come over here. I think I've found something." But Ty couldn't wait for him another minute as he slid his sword through his belt and headed into the cave with his star crystal in one hand and his shield by his side.

As he squeezed through that jagged crack, it led into a magnificent cave with brightly colored walls and columns of stone stretching up to the ceiling. Its dusty floor was as smooth as ice, and it looked like nothing had stepped foot inside there for hundreds of years.

The deeper he got, the more the walls started to sparkle like stars in the sky, lit up by the light of his star crystal. But when Ty walked up closer to get a better look, he got one huge surprise.

"Holy crap," muttered Ty as he slid his hand gently across the sparkling stones. "These walls are covered with thousands of diamonds, red rubies, and emeralds!"

He knew all the jewels in the world wouldn't be able to help his grandmother at all. He didn't come for diamonds or jewels; he was only interested in finding some blue fire rubies. Even so, Ty was no fool; he still grabbed the biggest and best jewels he could reach and filled his pockets until they bulged. "Dang, this is so cool," he thought to himself as he ran his fingers through the marble-sized stones.

With a huge grin, Ty continued through the cave and noticed a breeze of cold, damp air getting stronger and stronger. He knew there had to be another cave that led deeper into the crystal mountain somewhere close by. But as he approached the end of the cave, he found a tremendous pile of boulders sealing him inside. By the looks of it, Ty knew right away that there must have been a cave-in, and he figured the cave had to keep going on the other side. So he dropped to his knees and started digging as hard as he could to make his way through the wall of collapsed stone. But after a few minutes of moving some of the smaller rocks out of his way, he found a few massive boulders bigger than a bus hidden in the back.

Ty sat down and put his head in his hands, trying to come up with another idea. His heart was broken, and he was about to give up and try another cave when he saw a crevice in the ground leading deep into the dark shadows. Its crooked path ran along the back side of that shattered wall and disappeared into the darkness. That cave-in must have busted the floor wide open. When Ty knelt down and looked into that crevice, he could feel the cold air rushing up, and he could see that it led down into another cavern far below the mountain. This is what Ty was looking for—a secret passageway leading under the Crystal Mountain.

So, Ty looped his life leech rope to the closest boulder, slid through the crack, and started lowering himself down. Kicking off from the sheer wall like a mountain climber, he zipped down that crevice and discovered a massive cavern with steep, smooth walls dripping with sweet water next to a small river flowing across its rocky shore. "Wow, this place looks cool," he thought to himself as he held his light up high. The air was fresh and crisp, not musty and damp like all the others he had explored.

"There must be some blue fire rubies down here somewhere," Ty blurted out as he stared up at its high walls. "I can feel it."

He was so excited. He started sprinting along the river's

edge, looking up at the walls and trying to spot any sign of flickering blue light coming off those rubies. However, he wasn't paying much attention to where he was running as he tripped over a clump of dirt and fell face-first in the mud. The sound of that thump echoed through the cave over and over again like a dull quake.

With a little grin and a quick look around, he began to chuckle because he knew nobody was around to see him doing a face plant in the dirt. Then after picking his arrows back up that were scattered in front of him, he slid them back in his sleeve and slowly stood up. "That's gonna leave a mark," he mumbled as he rubbed his head and spit out a few gritty pieces of dirt. Slamming into the ground was a hard reminder that he had better be more careful down here.

As he brushed the last bit of the dirt off his face with his sleeve, he held his star crystal up and started walking more carefully. He followed that river for what seemed to be for miles, looking all around, behind fallen rocks and along the ceiling. But when he came up to the end of that cavern, it happened: glowing brightly, high up the rocky cliff wall, he spotted the biggest blue fire ruby he ever saw.

"Yahoo!" Ty screamed out as he started to dance around. "I knew I would find some! If I would've kept running, I would've missed it. There must be an angel watching over me today."

Ty was bursting with excitement. He ran straight up to that wall, threw his bow and arrows to the ground, and lept into action. It was the hardest thing he ever tried to climb in his life. The rocky cliff walls were dripping wet and covered with slippery green moss, but he took his time and studied every move he made. Inch by inch, he made his way up that treacherous wall, then when he reached out to grab his treasure, the rock he was holding on to started to pull loose. His eyes grew wide as he quickly reached out and latched onto a small lip in the wall just as the rock pulled out and went crashing to the ground below.

"That was way too close," he muttered as he struggled to find a good foothold.

Then as soon as he could steady himself, he took a deep

breath, reached out, and ripped that huge blue fire ruby out of that wall with his bare hands.

"I've got it. I can't believe it. I got one!"

With a grin as wide as the Shadow Forest itself, he climbed down as fast as he could and jumping the rest of the way when he got close to the ground.

Standing strong at the bottom of that wall, he wiped the sweat off his forehead and gazed into the glow of that blue fire ruby. He knew right away that it would be more than enough to help his grandmother, and there probably would be enough left over to help his dad too.

Ty didn't waste another second as he skipped over to the river's edge and cleaned off the sticky moss and mud, then wrapped it up and put it safely into his pouch. He knew he had a very long trip back home, and he wasn't about to lose it after all he's been through.

CHAPTER 7
THE BATTLE BELOW

Ty was so proud of what he had accomplished. He started to whistle as he jogged back. There was no better feeling in the world than the happiness Ty was feeling right now. He reached down and grabbed a cool skipping rock and sent it flying across that underground river. It skipped fourteen times and almost made it all the way across.

"Cool," muttered Ty while rummaging around for another. "This next one is going to be a record."

So after digging around for a couple of seconds, Ty spotted an awesome skipper. As he reached over to pick it up, an arrow came screaming next to his head and zipped into the river with an eerie thump.

"What the heck was that?" screamed Ty as he looked at the water, then back at the walls of the cavern.

Once again, the high-pitched sound of arrows in flight filled the air. "Oh no you don't!" shouted Ty as he snatched his shield and held up high just in time to stop three more arrows. Crack, crack, crack! Their sounds ripped through the darkness as they shattered like glass.

There was no way Ty was going to just stand there being a target. So he stood up boldly and pulled out his sword and shouted as loud as he could, "Whoever's firing these arrows at me had better stop right now and come out, or I'm coming in there after you!"

Ty held his sword high, ready for anything. All he could see were dark shadows and huge boulders scattered throughout the cavern's floor. But all of a sudden, one of those shadows seemed to flinch.

Ty readied his shield and shouted again, "I see you there, hiding behind that rock. If you don't throw down that bow and come out, I'm gonna come up there and pound you till your head falls off!"

Soft whispers drifted across the cavern floor as a shadowy figure crept between Ty and his only exit.

"Well, are you coming out, or do I have to come over there and pull you out?" ordered Ty.

Finally, after a few minutes had passed, a tall creature walked out from its hiding place and into the light of his star crystal. Although it walked like a man, it looked more like a lizard. It had big red eyes and light green scales covering it from head to toe. You could tell it was nervous because its long tail was twitching from side to side.

Ty looked over at that thing and roared out as loud as he could, "I don't know what your problem is, but if you shoot one more arrow at me, I'll shove it down your throat!"

Then in a very deep voice, like rumbling thunder, it slid its sword out from its sheath and bellowed at Ty. "Thief. You're a thief, and you're trespassing in the caves of the lost souls. My name is Torg, and I'm the keeper of the gates of Zintar. You're too small to be a rinog, and you don't smell like a Norgon, but you steal the blue stones from us, so you must be working for them."

Ty lowered his shield and looked all around in disbelief, "I don't know what you are talking about, but if you call me a thief one more time, I am going to break my foot off in your mouth!"

Torg looked at Ty and flicked his tail again. "If you're not working for the Norgons, then why did you steal from us? You can't lie to me! I watched you with my own eyes, pull the blue stone from the wall and put it in that pouch."

Ty pulled the blue fire ruby out of his pouch and handed it back to Torg. "Do you mean this thing here? Because if you do, I swear I didn't know that it belonged to anybody. I didn't know anybody lived down here, or I would've never come down here. I am not a thief, and I've never stolen anything in my life."

Torg snatched the stone right out of his hands, placed it on the rock shelf behind him, then waved his hand over his head as if to signal another guard that it was okay.

"You're not welcome here," snapped Torg as he stepped closer to Ty. "But since you gave it back and didn't try to lie about it, I'll let you live. Just remember, if you try to return here, I'll kill you."

Ty couldn't believe his ears. He finally found what he came for, but he had to give it right back. As Ty turned to walk away, he thought he should try at least one time to explain why he needed the stone. So he turned and called out, "Wait a minute, Torg. I've traveled a very long way for a blue fire ruby-like that one, and I desperately need it. Before I leave, I've gotta ask, would you like to trade or barter for it?"

Torg looked down at Ty, then folded his arms in front of himself. "What are you trying to pull?"

"I swear on my honor. I'm not trying to pull any trick on you. If you give me a chance, I'd like to trade what I have for that rock. You don't understand how far I traveled and how badly I need it. Please let me at least show you what I have."

Now Ty was a bit nervous, but he had nothing left to lose. So he reached into his pouch and pulled out some willow bark. "I have some powerful medicine that'll ease the pain when you get hurt, and I have some aloe plants that can help heal your wounds."

But by the look on Torg's face, he knew he wasn't very interested in what he had to offer.

"What you offer means nothing to me. I cannot barter with you. So leave now before I change my mind."

"Wait, I have more. I even have some precious gems that I found in the cavern above. You can have them all."

Torg just shook his head and pointed toward the way Ty came in. Ty looked down and checked his pockets, and the only thing he had left was a couple of those apples that he had picked right before he met Normack and a handful of berries.

"You can have these too. They're sweet apples and berries, and I picked them myself. I'm sorry, but this is all I have left. If it's not enough, I'll give you my sword and shield too. Please, Torg, it's all that I have."

Torg's eyes opened wide and his voice started to shake. "This is what you are offering in trade?" Torg muttered as he finally walked over and looked at what Ty was holding. "My job is to protect the gates of Zintar and all that belongs to it. I don't have the right to trade what does not belong to me, but I'll take your offer to the one who can. Stay here and don't move. I'll return with your answer."

Ty started fidgeting and kept his fingers crossed as he watched Torg walk away and disappear into the shadows on the far side of that cavern. But the whole time while Ty was waiting, the cave seemed to come alive with whispers and hushed voices. The longer he stood there, the more he noticed the creatures sneaking around in the shadows. It was starting to become a little creepy just standing there. After a few minutes, he saw Torg approaching from deep inside the cave, and he wasn't alone. There were four others with him.

Torg walked right up to Ty and in his deep growling voice, ordered him to bow his head because he was in the presence of her Majesty Queen Lylah, ruler of Zintar. It was very easy to figure out who Torg was talking about. Queen Lylah was a beautiful young girl draped in a long bright red robe and wearing three thick necklaces made of solid gold. Ty did just what he was told and bowed his head in respect.

Then Ty looked over at Torg and softly asked, "What did I do to be honored with a visit from her Majesty, Queen Lylah?"

That was when Queen Lylah slowly raised her hand and spoke with soft dignity and respect. "We do not get many visitors here, young man child. The ones that do venture into our lands are usually thieves and raiders that try to steal our treasures. My Royal Guardian told me that he watched you from the shadows as you took a stone that did not belong to you. Then he informed me that as you were trying to escape, he shot to protect my kingdom, but you did not shoot back. Instead, you returned the stone immediately and asked to trade for it. Is that true?"

"Yeah, that about sums it up, except he forgot to tell you that I didn't know anyone lived here. I am not looking for a fight or to steal from anybody. I'm just on a quest for my family."

Queen Lylah spoke out once more in her soft voice, "What you have offered us in payment for this stone is unacceptable. We could never make such a deal with you."

Ty was so disappointed he nearly started to cry. "I have nothing left to offer you of value. You see, that blue fire ruby I found is the only thing that will help my grandmother recover from her illness. So I'll give you anything if you would find it in your heart to trade with me."

Queen Lylah just smiled and walked next to Torg, "I can see that you are an honorable and noble creature, but there is no way I would ever trade that stone for what you are offering."

She raised her hand, and two huge guards lumbered out from the deep shadows of the cave and dragging a large black sack behind them, big enough that he could probably fit inside and tie up the top.

"Although those shiny stones are pretty, we have no need for them. You may have them back. But the willow, aloe, and fresh fruit you have offered are worth so much more than this small piece of a blue fire ruby. In turn, I will give you this sack of blue fire rubies in trade for what you have offered. That is if you still wish to trade with us."

Ty's jaw dropped to the ground as he stared at the huge sack. There were more blue fire rubies there than he had ever seen before. Its sides bulged out while the brittle sounds of crystals clinking together rang out as the guards placed it gently by his feet.

Queen Lylah looked into Ty's eyes and smiled, "My people are of noble blood. To accept your great offer for just one small ruby would too, be like stealing. I would like to make this fair for you and my people."

Ty was speechless; all he could do was stand there mumbling to himself. It was so unbelievable. There was enough in that sack to help his whole village while they fixed the cave at Eagle Cliff.

"Thank you, thank you, thank you," Ty muttered as he knelt down and looked at all she had offered him. "Thank you very much. You have no idea how wonderful this is. You've saved my grandmother's life and my village with your generosity."

Queen Lylah clapped her hands twice and waved her Guardians away, "The deal is done. I will send one of my Guardians with you. He will carry this for you and protect this sack with his life. There is only one thing you must know. I will only allow my guard to go with you as far as the opening to the caves of the lost souls. Then he must return, and you'll be on your own."

Ty told Queen Lylah that he thought sending one of her Royal Guardians to protect him was a great thing to do, and when he got to the clearing outside, his friend would be there, and together they would be just fine. But Ty couldn't stop thanking Queen Lylah for all she had done and vowed that he would return someday with a feast for her and her people in thanks for what she has done.

Queen Lylah smiled and held out her hand. "Take this ring. It holds the royal seal of Zintar if you so choose to return. All you have to do is show my Guardian this ring. You'll be protected from any harm and be treated as my royal guest."

Ty bowed his head and thanked her once more, then turned and started to make his way back to the surface with the prize of a lifetime.

"Wait, Ty, do not forget your pretty stones," Torg grunted as he started to grin. "You said they were special to you, so do not forget them."

Ty turned back and blushed a little bit. "I almost forgot. I did want to give them to my Mom and dad. They would love to have them."

Torg bent down, scooped them up, and gently filled Ty's

pouch. "Then they should have them. Now let's go. We have stayed here by the river too long already. The Norgon's never pass up an easy target, and we are standing in one of their hunting grounds."

CHAPTER 8
SURPRISE IN THE DARKNESS

Ty was bursting with excitement. He had more blue fire rubies than he could have wished for.

Torg turned to Queen Lylah respectfully, "With your permission, since this creature acted with respect and honor towards me, I wish to serve as his protector and join you're Guardian in carrying out your wishes that he safely arrives with the stones through the caves of lost souls."

Queen Lylah nodded her head, granting Torg's wishes, and chose her strongest Guardian, Commander Scales, to carry the sack of blue fire rubies.

Torg couldn't help but smile because the other Guardian was his good buddy. Even though Commander Scales was quite a bit bigger than Torg, he had this long scar across his face from a battle against a Norgon warlord. All the Zintarian guards knew and respected him because he was one of the toughest and meanest Guardians ever to wear the mark of the Queen's personal guards.

Scales just looked over his shoulder at Torg and gave him a sneaky little smirk, then snatched the sack of rubies right off the ground with one hand, slung it over his shoulder with a rattling thud, and stepped proudly beside him and stood at attention. "I am honored to go, my Queen. I will carry your gift proudly and protect it as you commanded."

Then Torg and Scales knelt on one knee respectfully to Queen Lylah, stood back up, and turned to walk away.

Scales looked back at Ty with a grin on his face. "Are you coming?"

Ty turned back to Queen Lylah, bowed deeply, and smiled, "Thank you again, Your Majesty. I'll never forget your kindness."

All three turned sharply and headed along the river's edge, and disappeared back into the darkness. Even with two strong Guardians to lead him back through the cavern, it was still a bit creepy there with the flutter of bats flying high in the cavern and the sound of the river splashing against the rocky shore.

But Scales took the lead right away, and Torg walked a few paces behind him. They were marching like true soldiers, stride for stride, in perfect step. As they made their way deeper into the cavern, Ty couldn't figure out how they knew which way to go, but somehow, they did. It really didn't bother him too much because he was headed out with his prize, and at the pace they were going, he would be back outside in no time at all.

As they walked along the shore of that underground river, Ty was so happy that he started to pick up some stones and hurl them across the river while humming a little marching song in the rhythm of their steps.

"What do you think you are doing?" grumbled Torg as he slapped his tail against the ground. "You're making such a big racket. Every creature around is going to hear us coming."

"What are you worried about? There's nothing around down here but bats and spiders."

"Hush up, you two," whispered Scales. "I don't want to break up your conversation, but you guys had better quiet down. Those two pillars of iron ore over there mark the edge of the Norgons' territory, and I don't feel like fighting off an army right now."

"Wait just one minute," Ty whispered as he snuck up next to Scales. "Torg didn't say anything about Norgons before. What's a Norgon? And what do you mean about fighting off an army?"

Scales stopped, turned to Ty, and shook his head. "Norgons are vicious creatures that travel in packs, just like wolves. They live by scavenging and plundering anything they can get their claws on. It is hard to hear them coming because they ride on the backs of wild cave rats. I've fought them many times, and they're strong and very sneaky, and I've walked through the scattered bits of flesh and bones after an attack. The lucky ones are killed by spears or arrows while those who survive are fed to their pets."

"They ride rats? What do these things look like?"

Torg looked over at Ty and tried to explain, "You just don't get it, do you? A full-grown Norgon warrior could stand four or five feet tall. They have incredibly thick armor and a nasty attitude to go with it. If that's not bad enough, they look more like huge insects, almost like a praying mantis, with poisonous spikes on their backs and large eyes like a fly. They're hard to kill, and they never stop attacking even after you hack off a couple of their legs. Now, do you understand? We should move quickly and keep quiet!"

Ty didn't say another word. He just nodded his head and grasped his sword tightly. He remembered his last encounter with a cave rat, and they were nothing to play around with.

Torg looked at Scales and pointed behind him, "Considering you are carrying that heavy sack, you should take the rear and I'll take the lead. That way, we will be able to move quickly if anything happens."

Ty pushed his way ahead and interrupted them again, "Listen you two. I didn't see a thing when I walked through here earlier. I don't think there're any of these Norgon things around. So let's just keep going."

But it was a bit too late. Their voices had already echoed throughout the cave and caught the attention of a rogue Norgon scout as it crept silently above their heads on a rocky ledge, studying their every move.

Fortunately, this Norgon scout was very young and alone. So it didn't dare attack. It just stayed in the shadows, waiting and watching.

Torg and Scales knew it was a very dangerous place, so they stayed alert and cautious as they continued along the trail that Ty left when he first got there. Meanwhile, slowly closing in on them from behind, was a squad of Norgon warriors with one thing on their mind—food.

Torg and Scales weren't Guardians of Zintar for nothing. They were sharp and courageous warriors trained for combat from birth.

Scales stopped right where he was and gripped his spear tightly, whispering, "Shhhh, I think I hear something."

"I think I hear something too," whispered Ty as he crouched down low, studying the shadows behind them. "It sounds like it's coming from back there."

Torg and Scales looked at each other with dark and determined eyes. Quickly, Scales looked around and pointed to the cavern's wall. In a flash, he tossed the sack of blue fire rubies behind a stone pillar and started to wipe their tracks clean while Torg led Ty to a safe hiding spot right behind a large crystal pillar jutting out from the ground next to the wall.

"Here they come," whispered Scales, pointing into the shadows. "Get that man child safe." Then just as the Norgons came into sight, Scales tossed a handful of paka root to hide their scent and finished covering their tracks.

"Hurry," snapped Torg as he franticly waved. "I can see them from here."

Scales ducked down as low as he could and dove behind the pillar, then drew his bow.

"We'll stay hidden right here, Ty," whispered Torg, "and wait for them to pass by. But if we have to fight, this will be a good place to defend ourselves."

It didn't take long until Ty had his first look at a Norgon warrior. There must have been a dozen of them scurrying along the shoreline, riding on the backs of the biggest cave rats he had ever seen while a dozen foot soldiers followed close behind.

"They look like some kind of evil aliens," whispered Ty as he poked his head up. "I hope they don't see us. All I want to do is get back home. I don't want to fight those things."

"We'll get you home," muttered Torg defiantly. "We just have to hide out here for a little while until those things move off."

Torg, Scales, and Ty watched as the hunting party stopped right below them and jumped off those nasty beasts. The cave rats had leathery saddles strapped to their backs and thick chains around their necks for the Norgon to use as reins to control them.

Torg tried as hard as he could to keep Ty safely hidden, but he just kept peeking around the side of that pillar to watch them as they scurried around the shoreline, trying to pick up their trail. They buzzed and clicked like locusts to each other while stabbing their spears furiously into the water as if they had seen something in its wake.

When the three Norgons that were riding the bigger rats in the back of the pack finally arrived, they stood around in the center of the beach and studied everything in sight. After a few minutes, the largest one—with a big chunk of its right claw missing—reached out and waived its spear high above its head and made a terrible screech.

It took only seconds until Ty figured out what that thing had meant as the foot soldiers ran back and released the rats they had chained down. Scales must have known what that thing was doing too, because he grabbed Ty by his shoulder to pull him back into the shadows safely behind him and Torg.

"Stay very quiet and very still," whispered Scales. "They're releasing their rats to hunt us down. If they don't pick up our scent, they should leave soon. I scattered some paka root across our tracks. That should keep us safe."

Ty's heart started pounding as he remembered how scared he was when his father told him wild stories about the Shadow Forest. Then suddenly, a quiet calm flowed through his body. He was no longer afraid. He knew he didn't want to fight, but he was ready to fight if he had to. He took his first step in becoming a true warrior.

They calmly watched in silence as those rats scurried in all directions. Back and forth they went, sniffing and scratching the rocky shoreline for any fresh scent. Ty clenched his sword tight and watched as one of the smaller rats started digging around where he once stood. Squealing and hopping madly, it shoved its nose deep into the ground as two more rats joined in, ripping the area apart.

Scales and Torg kept tapping each other, pointing and nodding, watching and planning as the Norgons fanned out in their desperate search.

The Norgons and their disgusting rats scoured the whole beach from the water's edge to the cavern's wall, but they never picked up any sign of our friends.

Scales started to grin because he knew his trick worked as that hunting party started to gather back at the river's edge. Then with a loud screech, one of the leaders jumped on its rat and started to ride back where they came from. Scales and Torg lowered their bows and let out a soft sigh of relief.

But that's when their luck ran out. That lone scout hiding above their heads stood up and let out the most awful screech you've ever heard, then pointed right at them, giving their position away.

"So much for hiding, Torg!" yelled Scales. "I prefer to do this the old-fashioned way: shoot first and then shoot again."

Torg let out a powerful growl, then stood up and sent an arrow screeching through the air. Smack! His arrow sank deep into its target, sending that creature tumbling off its rat and splashing into the rushing water. The whole cavern lit up with the sounds of Norgons screeching and scurrying to find cover.

Zip, zip, zip! The Norgon fired back wildly with a barrage of arrows.

"Watch out!" screamed Torg, knocking Ty to the ground as an arrow sliced by his head. "If you get the smallest scratch from one of those, you'll be dead in seconds. They're dipped in poison!"

Shot after shot, Torg and Scales kept the hordes of vicious monsters pinned down. However, they didn't come prepared for a ferocious battle against a whole squad of Norgon warriors. They were running out of arrows fast.

But Ty wasn't about to stay out of the fight. As soon as Torg turned his head, he grabbed his bow and sent an arrow screaming across the cavern, then splashing into the river below.

"I said get down and stay down!" yelled Torg. "Remember, it's my job to make sure you leave here in one piece, and I'm gonna do just that."

"Are you kidding?" he shouted back as he flicked Torg's hand off his shoulder. "You're totally outnumbered, and you need my help. If I don't start helping, none of us is gonna make it. Now stand back and watch this!"

Quick as lightning, Ty drew another arrow and fired his bow again. This time his shot bounced across the beach and skipped across the water like a skipping stone and landed in the water with a hollow kerplunk.

"What do you think you're doing?" Shouted Torg as he ducked out of the way of another shot. "The Norgons are the ones running around on the beach. So stop shooting the water!"

"I'm trying," shouted Ty as he readied his bow again. "But my fingers slipped!"

Torg was furious and shoved Ty out of the way again. "We don't have enough arrows for you to keep shooting the river."

Ty just ignored him, then gritted his teeth and shot again. This time, his arrow sent an eerie squeal as it zipped through the cavern just before it skipped across the shore on the far side of the river.

"You've got to be kidding me?" shouted Torg as he watched it slide to a stop. "You just shot the water again!" He bellowed out as he threw his bow on the ground.

"I didn't mean it. My fingers slipped again." snapped Ty as he reached for another arrow. "I'll get one this time. Just watch."

"This ain't target practice little man child!" roared Torg as he grabbed Ty's bow and snapped it in half. "If you wanna help, then stay out of the way, or throw some rocks!"

Ty just sat down and leaned back against the wall and just sat there muttering in disgust. He realized he couldn't hit the side of a house with that bow he made, and there was nothing he could do about it.

That's when he looked down and started to grin. His eyes were filling with rage as the Norgon's arrows kept slamming against the wall they were hiding behind.

"Make every shot count," shouted Torg as loud as thunder. "Send that horde to their ancestors!"

Shot after shot, Torg and Scales kept fighting as the Norgons scurried around in circles and continued to shoot back.

"Wait, I've got a plan!" shouted Ty as he gave scales a shove in his back. "Let's do this together."

As scales drew back to fire once more, Ty stood up and flung a rock as hard as he could and smacked a rat rider right off its rat.

"Good shot," snickered Scales as he sent an arrow right in the chest of the rat rider as it tried to get up.

"I'm almost out of arrows," shouted Scales as he sank another deep into the chest of a charging cave rat.

"Me too," bellowed Torg as he dove out of the way as an arrow nearly hit him in his throat.

"This ain't gonna work for much longer," shouted Ty as he threw another rock into the swirling horde. "We've gotta make a break for it soon before we get murdered."

Scales knew they would never survive if they tried to run. Those Norgons moved too fast riding on those greasy rats, and there was no cover to hide behind for at least a hundred yards. They had no choice. They had to fight it out right now before that lone scout could return with more troops.

"Are you guys ready," shouted Ty? "Cause I'm getting real tired of these jokers trying to kill us. So grab your swords and follow me. It's payback time."

Ty drew his sword and gripped his shield. He wasn't about to take it anymore. It was go time.

With a thunderous battle cry that echoed throughout the cave, Ty charged out from behind that crystal pillar and headed straight for three Norgon warriors. Blocking arrows with his shield and jumping across two dead cave rats, he slashed his way into the heart of the Norgon's hoard.

Torg and Scales were right behind him, chopping and hacking their way across the cave. Their sudden attack caught them by surprise as they tried to draw their swords.

Ty, Scales, and Torg fought like a hurricane ripping through a forest of paper trees—moving across the cave and attacking every warrior in sight until the last one finally fell.

Torg looked over at Ty and slapped him in his back with a loud pop, "You fight like a true Guardian, but remember, if anybody is going to give the order to charge, it'll be me. And don't ever forget that!" Then turning to Scales, he added, "Now that's the last of them. We better get out of here before more start coming. I'll pick up some of these arrows, and you grab the rubies, and then let's get going."

Scales looked back at Ty and whispered over his shoulder to Torg, "That kid's got guts, Commander."

"You're right, and if he tries another stunt like that again, we might get a chance to see them lying across the ground!" he replied in a low, sarcastic tone.

"Young warrior," snapped Torg as he walked over the body of a rat. "Hurry up and grab as many arrows as you can, and be careful not to scratch yourself. After a fight like that, I would hate to lose you because you were careless. And grab yourself one of their bows and take one of their quivers too. The one next to that rat rider should prove to be an improvement over that stick of yours!"

Ty nodded his head and started running around, picking up as many arrows as he could find. After a battle like that, he grabbed as much as he could. But while Ty was gathering up every arrow he could get his hands on, Scales charged back to the cavern's wall, snatched that sack of rubies from behind the pillar, and threw it over his shoulder.

"Let's go! Move it! Move it! Move it!" shouted Torg like a drill sergeant to his troops. "We've already stayed here too long!"

CHAPTER 9
THE ATTACK OF THE RINOG

It was amazing how quickly they made it back to where Ty's rope was hanging. When Torg and Scales saw that rope hanging there, they stopped right in their tracks.

Torg looked over at Ty, then shook his head. "Zintarians don't climb ropes, but don't worry. We're the best climbers in the worlds above and below. We'll climb up the cliff face instead."

Ty just smiled and shook his head, realizing that, since those two were part lizard, climbing straight up a cavern wall should be no big deal for them.

"No problem," snickered Ty as he looked at their razor-sharp claws. "I think it would be a lot easier if we just tie the sack to the end of my rope and pulled it up when we get there."

"Yes, I agree," Torg grunted and then tied the satchel tightly to the end of the rope. "We'll pull it up after you climb up. It shouldn't take too long."

Ty looked around and started to get that sneaky little grin on his face again. You could tell right away that he was up to something.

"Hey, I bet you I can make it to the top before you two can."

"Only a fool would bet a Zintarian to a climbing race!" laughed Scales, slapping Torg across his back.

"Oh, are you scared that you'll lose?" replied Ty with a smirk from ear to ear.

"You're on," snapped Torg as his tail flicked anxiously. "And if we win, you must carry the sack all the way out to the opening of the caves of the lost souls while we escort you."

"Okay, you got it. The loser carries the bag for the rest of the way."

-Ty wanted to beat those two to the top of the cave real bad. He figured he would have a real good chance because they had a long way to go, and it was going to be a really hard climb, even for them.

"Get ready, set, and go," yelled Scales.

"Holy smokes!" Ty muttered as he watched those two take off running across the cave, disappearing in a wisp of dust. "Those two are super-fast!"

Ty jumped over the sack, snatched the rope, and started to climb as fast as he could. When he was about halfway up, Ty peeked over at Torg and Scales and couldn't believe what he saw. They weren't having any problems climbing up that cave wall at all. In fact, they looked like a couple of squirrels running up a tree. The race was definitely on.

But Ty wasn't about to give up. He wanted to show those two he was a strong climber too. He knew he had an edge on them, not because he the best rope climber in school but because those guys had to race across the floor, then up the wall, and finally make their way past a skinny opening.

So Ty pulled and pulled as hard as he could. He climbed so hard his hands started to turn red, and his arms started to burn. Before long, he reached the top of the cliff and started to wiggle and pull his way through the jagged crack in the floor. With his muscles burning and his hands throbbing,

Ty spun around, grabbed the rope, and started to pull that heavy sack up.

Torg and Scales must have had some trouble coming up because Ty had that sack safely on the ground next to him, and they still weren't anywhere around. So he grabbed his rope, coiled it back up, and slung it around his shoulder with a prize-winning grin.

Totally exhausted, Ty plopped down on the edge of the cliff and swung his feet over the side, giggling with excitement. He knew he just beat the pants off those two. With every muscle in his body burning like fire, he just sat there, resting, barely able to move at all. After a few seconds, Ty felt one of them reach down and pick up the sack behind him.

"What happened to you two? You get lost or something? I thought you guys would have been here already," laughed Ty as he flipped a rock down the hole. "Now, which one of you are going to carry my sack the rest of the way out?"

When Ty looked over his shoulder and saw Scales and Torg running right towards him from the back of the cave with their bows in their hands, he started scratching his head.

"Get down, Ty! Get down!" ordered Scales as he leaped over a large boulder.

"What the heck?" muttered Ty as he stood up and slowly peered over his shoulder. But as soon as he turned his head, he found himself face-to-face with a huge rinog. Its hot and smelly breath blew his hair back as he stood there, frozen with fear.

"Hey now big fella, I don't want any trouble. But that's my sack you have in your hands, and you're not leaving here with it. So please give it back."

Just as soon as the last word left his mouth, that big thing reached back and clobbered Ty so hard he flew all the way across the cave and smashed into the wall on the other side.

Torg and Scales sent their arrows screaming through the cave right into that rinog's chest. Smack! Smack! You could hear the sound echoing across the cave as they hit their mark and shattered like glass. They fired again and again, but their arrows only kept splintering against its thick gray hide.

"Get behind me, Ty," yelled Torg. "I'll protect you!"

Ty lay there a little dazed for a few seconds and then slowly sat up. It was amazing that horrendous punch didn't kill him, but his armor was strong, and that hit only made him mad. He reached back, drew an arrow, and fired. You could hear the loud crack ring out as Ty's arrow hit that rinog right in the back of its head.

"I told you that I didn't want any trouble. But if you think you're gonna leave here with my stuff, you've got another thing coming!" yelled Ty as he sent another one screaming across the cavern.

But I guess that rinog wanted that sack really bad because it let out a terrible roar and charged with all its might. Ty stood up, clenched his fists, and then slung his bow back over his shoulder. "If you think you're man enough, then bring it on!"

Torg and Scales couldn't believe their eyes. Nobody had ever picked a fight against a rinog before. Everyone knows that only a full-grown vipercon would have a chance against a charging rinog.

"Don't be stupid and just stand there!" yelled Torg. "Get out of there and climb as high as you can. We'll try to distract it. Now go."

Ty heard the whistle of arrows screaming by and smashing right into that rinog's neck, but they were just kept snapping like twigs.

"Run, Ty. Get out of there!" Scales hollered.

But Ty just stood his ground, not flinching an inch. Closer and closer, that huge beast came. The ground started to shake, and chunks of the rock wall started crumbling to the ground.

"Look out!" screamed Torg.

But it was too late; that rinog was running full blast, and it was just a few feet away from pounding a mudhole in Ty.

Then just as it lowered its head, Ty sprung into action. Fast as lightning, He grabbed that monster by its ears and flipped him over his shoulder and sending it hurtling across the cave. The cave burst with a tremendous roar as the rinog sailed through the air.

"Watch out, Scales!" Screamed Torg as he tumbled out of the way seconds before it slammed into the crystal pillar they were standing next to, sending large chunks of rock and crystals flying everywhere with a mighty crash.

Ty sprinted across the cave and jumped on top of a busted-up piece, then shouted out again. "How do you like being tossed across a cave? It kind of hurts, don't it? Now drop that sack right now and get out of here, or I'm going to teach you a lesson about stealing that you'll never forget!"

Torg watched with his mouth hanging open while a cloud of rock dust swirled across the floor as that rinog laid flat on its face. It stayed there dazed for a few seconds, then struggled as it tried to stand. But when it finally made it back on its feet, and it looked over at Ty, the veins in its massive arms started to throb, and its gray face turned beet red with fury.

"Well, what are you waiting for?" shouted Ty as he drew his sword. "Are you gonna put my stuff down, or do you want some more?"

That was all it could stand. It went into a furious rage. With a deafening roar, it charged right at Ty, swinging wildly and pounding massive stone columns into dust as it quickly closed in.

Scales and Torg kept shooting their bows, trying to give Ty some time to get away from its deadly rampage. But he just stood there again, watching as it got closer and closer. He knew it was no use trying to run, so he readied his shield and slowly swung his sword to his side as he gritted his teeth. This time, he was ready for him.

With an explosion that rocked the cave, they clashed head-on. Dust was flying and the walls were shaking as Ty went hand-to-hand with it. All you could see were glimpses of Ty swinging his sword and blocking that beast's mighty blows with his shield as a cloud of dust filled the room.

Torg threw down his bow, then grabbed his knife and dove right into that fight. But he never stood a chance; he had no armor or shield to protect him.

He pounced on that rinog's back and grabbed it by its horn. While pulling back as hard as he could, he slammed his blade into its neck, but its hide was so thick it just bounced off and didn't even leave a scratch.

"Let go of him, you jerk, or I'll rip your head off!" boasted Torg, throwing his knife to the ground and grabbing it with both hands.

Its head flung back as Torg strained with all his might. "I've got him. Grab the rubies, Scales!"

But Scales was too busy joining the fight. He dove into the dust-filled air headfirst, landing on its chest, grabbed its arm, and started prying it back. Fuming with anger, it let out a tremendous roar, drew back its fist, and clobbered Scales with a lucky shot, sending him tumbling across the floor and over the edge of the cliff.

"No!" Torg screamed as he turned and watched his friend disappear into the blackness.

Seconds later, the hollow sound of Scales' body slamming into the ground at the bottom of the cliff crept across the floor like a cold winter's wind.

Torg let go of that rinog's horn with one hand and started punching it in the face as hard as he could.

But when it realized Torg let go with one hand, it swung its head around and bashed him with his horn, sending him flying across the room and into a crystal pillar. His body flopped to the ground, all twisted and still.

Ty was furious and lost all control. He threw his shield down in the dirt, and with his sword held high, he charged in a screaming blind rage.

The rinog kicked up a wave of dust as it lowered its head and charged back at Ty. The only ones left standing were seconds away from a devastating impact.

Ty leaped into the air and came down on that rinog's head with a mighty chop from his sword. Smack! But his attack wasn't enough to slow it down one bit.

That rinog unleashed his fury and slammed into Ty with the force of a freight train. It dug its horn deep across his chest and smashed him so hard he flew across the cave, hitting the ceiling before coming crashing down to the floor below.

Ty and Torg were both lying face-first in the dirt, covered with dust and busted rock, and barely breathing.

The rinog let out a hideous growl as it stood there gazing down at our two friends as the dust swirled across the floor.

It took a few moments until they could open their eyes, dazed and seeing stars. After a knockdown drag-out fight like that, neither one could move at all. All they could do was lie there helplessly and watch as the rinog ran away and disappeared into the blackness with his prize.

Ty rolled over, shook Torg, and mumbled, "Scales. We got to help Scales!"

With every ounce of energy, they crawled back to the edge of the ravine and looked down. Scales was lying there face down on a pile of rocks. "Is he dead?" Ty whispered.

"No, he can't be. He can't be dead. He's just knocked out or something."

Torg didn't bother going back to the side of the cliff to climb down safely; he just reached over and dug his claws into the cold hard stone and slid down, leaving a jagged line of claw marks in the stone wall. Then Ty flung his rope over the edge and followed him down.

"Scales, get up," ordered Torg. "You can't let that thing beat you. I won't allow it!"

Torg bent down and gently turned Scales over. He was still breathing. "Did you get the rubies back?" mumbled Scales as blood dripped from the corner of his mouth. "Is Ty all right?"

"Ty's fine. He right here. But that rinog got away with the blue fire rubies."

"You've got to get them back, Torg. The Queen, she was counting on us."

"Don't worry, my friend. I'll get them back. Can you make it back to Zintar?"

Scales slowly sat up and leaned against the wall. "Yes, yes. I'll be all right. Now go and get them back. That's an order."

"Let's go," barked Torg.

"Are you nuts? We can't just leave him here like this. Forget the rubies. We've gotta help him."

"I'll be okay, Ty. I've had worse falls than that when I was young. So just get going, and Torg, I'll inform the Queen that you will not be returning until Ty's gift is back safely in his hands. Now go, the both of you, and may the winds of luck be with you!"

Torg and Ty nodded their heads in silence and started to climb back up. This time, they went very slowly as they struggled inch by inch. Their bodies were weak and battered, but they just kept on climbing.

Finally, after struggling to pull themselves over the edge of the wall, they collapsed on the ground, exhausted and gasping for breath. After few minutes passed, Ty looked over at Torg and took a deep breath, "Where in the world did that thing come from, and could you please explain to me how it was able to walk right up behind me without making a sound?"

"I don't know where it came from, but rinogs are known for their stealth when they hunt. What I want to know is, what in the world were you thinking of challenging a full-grown rinog to a fistfight? Are you nuts? You know the only thing that could stop a rinog is a vipercon."

"I'm not an idiot. I know only a vipercon can bring down a rinog," he mumbled as he kept rubbing his head. "At least I had my sword and my armor to protect me. When you jumped on that rinog's back with a dull knife, I thought you were either the bravest person I've ever known or the stupidest one ever born. But at least I slowed it down, and if you don't believe me, then maybe you can explain how I got its blood on my sword."

"What, let me see that," sputtered Torg as he snatched his sword out of his hands. "That's impossible. No weapon ever created has ever cut a rinog! You must have cut yourself."

"I didn't cut myself. My blood is red, not blue. I hit that thing as hard as I could, but all I could do was scratch him up a little bit."

"I vowed to help you get your stuff back, but I don't want to get killed. So next time you feel like picking a fight, why don't you pick on something only twice your size?" snickered Torg as he slapped him on the back of his head. "Now if you're done bragging, we gotta get moving before that thing gets away."

"Just try to relax," Ty chuckled with a big grin on his face as he stood up then started brushing the dust off of his shirt. "I'm not too worried about that monster getting away. As big as that thing is, we won't have any problem tracking it down. The first thing we have to do when we get out of here is to find my friend and tell him what happened. Then we can go after that thief and get my stuff back. Trust me. When you meet Normack, you'll understand why that thing won't stand a chance!"

"I don't know who Normack is but have you thought about what we're going to do when we catch up with that thing? I mean, do you have a plan on how we are going to get that sack away from him?"

Ty just shrugged his shoulders while they walked away, "I have no idea. I'm just making it up as I go along.

Torg just shook his head and didn't say another word. All he kept thinking about was how he had failed his Queen and what he was going to do when he saw that rinog again.

Hey, Torg, I think that's the entrance to the cave is up ahead. I never thought I would be so glad to get outside. Just look at that beautiful sunlight, so warm and bright."

CHAPTER 10
THE ALLIANCE IS COMPLETE

Ty had to cover his eyes as he left the cave. The sun was stunningly bright, and it took a while for his eyes to get used to it. Torg, on the other hand, had to take it kind of slow since he lived all his life deep underground, and the only light he knew came from star crystals. He had to stay in the shadows of the cave for a few minutes longer while his eyes stopped burning.

"Now come on out here," Ty shouted as he danced around. "The sun feels great."

"This is incredible," Torg muttered as he walked into the sunlight. "I've heard stories about the outside, but I never thought it could be so huge and beautiful. How big is this cave you call outside? I can't even see any walls, and where is the ceiling?"

"There are no walls or ceilings out here. That's why it is called the outside dummy. You have a lot to learn, my friend."

Torg was spellbound at everything he could see. Ty taught him about the trees and grass, the clouds, and the sky. The world was full of wonder and beauty that Torg had never seen before. It was like showing the world to a child for the first time.

"This is my world," Ty boasted with a huge smile. "They're more creatures and animals out here than you could possibly imagine. So be careful and watch your step."

As they walked around the side of the Crystal Mountain, Ty was showing Torg the birds and small creatures that lived all around them.

"I don't believe it," Ty mumbled as he stopped and crossed his arms in front of himself. "Would you look at that? While we were in that nasty cave, fighting Norgons and getting slammed by a rinog, Normack was just lying around up here getting a suntan."

Torg looked all around and turned to Ty with a puzzled look on his face. "I don't see anybody anywhere."

"He's right over there, all coiled up like a little baby next to that boulder that kind looks like a hammer. Hey, sleepyhead, wake up. I wanna introduce you to a friend of mine!"

Normack slowly raised his head, then looked over to Ty, "It's about time you got back from that cave, fish feet. I thought you got lost down there. Now, where's your little friend that you want me to meet?"

When Torg looked over and got a good look at who Ty was talking to, his eyes popped opened wide with fear; he didn't know if he should run or fight.

"I don't believe it; you've got to be kidding me!" muttered Torg as he slowly started to back away. "Please tell me that you are not talking about that vipercon over there?"

"Well, sure I am," laughed Ty as he gave Torg a nudge. "He's a really good guy once you get to know him, just as long as he doesn't try to eat you like he tried to eat me the first time we met. But don't worry. Since he ate a big cave rat a little while ago, I don't think you will have anything to worry about. Just do yourself a favor and don't get too close to him because his breath could kill a rinog from thirty feet away."

"Well then, if he is a friend of yours, then he's a friend of mine."

Then Torg worked up some courage and introduced himself to Normack, face-to-face.

"You were in that cave all morning. I was afraid you might have gotten lost. What in the world were you doing in there for all that time? Did you find any fire rubies?"

"Normack, you got to believe me. It was incredible. I had enough blue fire rubies to help everybody in my whole village. But we ran into a little problem, a real nasty problem."

That's when Ty told him the whole story about Queen Lylah, Torg, and Scales and what that rinog did with his rubies.

Normack stood straight up and stared into the Shadow Forest, "That must've been the same rinog that came bursting out of the cave about half an hour ago. I don't know what you two did to that thing, but it ran out of there so fast I nearly shed my skin. He went over that hill next to those cliffs, heading straight for the lost meadows. It shouldn't be too hard to find him because he was knocking down anything that stood in his way."

Torg jumped up and drew his sword. "What are you two waiting for? That stinking slimeball is trying to get away, and I would like to teach that brute a lesson about stealing that he'll never forget."

"Sounds great to me," hissed Normack, looking back at Torg. "I hate a thief."

Ty looked around with a huge smile on his face. "Well, guys, the schools are open, and I don't think a note from the teacher is going to be enough. So let's catch up to that jerk and take back what he stole, and if he don't like it, I guess he's in for the pounding of his life."

Torg knelt on one knee and drew an arrow on the ground surrounded by some weird symbols.

"Okay, I am ready now," Torg said softly as he began walking back to where they were standing. "Let's get going."

"What was that all about?" Ty asked while trying to peek around him.

"I needed to leave a message for Scales in case he tries to follow us. This will let him know where we are going and what we plan to do."

"Whatever," snapped Ty. "If you're done playing in the sand, I have some payback to dish out, and we are losing daylight."

Nobody said a word as they turned and followed that trail deep into the Shadow Forest. This was the first time in history that anyone had ever tried to track down a full-grown rinog. Ty and Torg both knew, deep down in their souls, that they were lucky to be alive after that pounding they got inside the cave. But to survive a second battle would take a lot more than luck.

"Let's try to pick up some speed," Torg commanded as he started jogging. "That monster had at least a good hour head start and is probably miles away from us right now."

"Hold on," shouted Ty as he waved Torg back. "That's probably true, but I have a better idea how we can find out for sure. Hey, Normack, can you slither up to the top of those trees and try to see how far away that thing might be? If he starts heading toward the valley, we might be able to cut him off by crossing over those hills up ahead."

"That sounds like a great idea," hissed Normack as he slithered straight up a large tree next to the trail. You couldn't hear a sound, not even the crackle of a single leaf as he disappeared into the branches of that tree like a whisper in the night.

"Your friend moves like a Ghost," grunted Torg as he leaned against the side of the tree. "But even for him, it's gonna take him a while to make it up to the top of that tree."

"You're right about that," Ty snickered as he sat down in the grass. "While we wait, do you mind if I ask you something?"

"No, not at all. What do you want to know?"

"Well, I was just kind of curious about what you think of the outside so far."

"Are you kidding? Your world is so amazing! I just don't understand why those creatures invade our caves and smash our homes like they do. We never go to the surface and try to destroy their world. That's why I don't understand why it has attacked my people for all these years. You have seen our world. It isn't full of beautiful riches as far as your eyes can see like your world is."

"Well, I don't know why those things have been stealing from your people for all those years. But it's gonna stop as soon as I can get my hands on him. He's gonna wish he had never gone into that cave," boasted Ty as he walked next to the tree and looked up, trying to spot Normack. "Well, that was quick. Normack's coming back down. I hope he's got some good news."

"How in the world do you know that?"

"Well, it's pretty easy," laughed Ty as he took a couple steps back. "The stench of dead rats is getting closer."

"That's not very funny," hissed Normack from the branches just above their heads. "I need you two to listen very closely because I have some bad news. I know which way that rinog is headed. Grab your weapons and prepare yourselves for battle because you're not going to like where it's headed."

CHAPTER 11
THE SAVAGE ATTACK

After all Ty had been through, there wasn't anything at all that was going to scare him now. So he checked his sword and shield, looked at Torg and Normack, and smiled. Normack was well aware that whenever he smiled like that, you knew it meant trouble. If that rinog knew what was good for him, he would drop that sack and disappear into the forest before those three caught up to him.

Ty walked up to Normack and placed his hand on his side. "Whatever it is, I'm sure it won't be that bad. Wherever it's gone couldn't possibly be worse than the places we've been. So don't keep it a secret, tell us."

"You don't understand!" Normack hissed loudly as he slid down and coiling up next to him. "That rinog is still about a half-hour ahead of us and crushing everything in its path. He's headed straight for a village next to a river. Unfortunately, that village is surrounded by a hedge of razor bushes.

"You've gotta be kidding me!" screamed Ty, raising his arm and pointing the other way. "You gotta be wrong! My village must be miles from here, and it's in that direction!"

Normack raised straight up and flicked his tongue hard, "Look, the Crystal Mountain is to the north, and the swamps are to the east, which means we have traveled in a huge circle. We're almost back to the place where you started. That thing is headed straight for your home, and there's nothing in its way to stop it."

"Normack, we got to stop that thing before it reaches my home. They won't stand a chance! I need your help," Ty begged as he paced around in a circle. "I'm not fast enough to catch up with that rinog before he gets to my village. Please carry me on your back. I know I promised never to ask that again, but without your help, I'll never make it back in time. You can make it there faster than I can. Please, Normack, help me save my village."

"You want to ride on my back like a horse? I am a vipercon, lord of the Shadow Forest, and I don't give piggyback rides," hissed Normack in a furious rage.

Ty was crushed as he looked around in despair.

Normack glanced over at Torg, slithered right up to Ty and whispered, "Since you have risked your life for me and you have fought to protect others, I would be honored to give you a lift across this treacherous land. But I am afraid that wouldn't work. Your arms are too short and you would fall off and get killed if I traveled fast as the wind."

Ty stood there for a moment because he knew Normack was right. That's when Ty got a great idea. He took out his sword, sliced off a chunk of his rope, and started to twist it and tie it in knots. As he was finishing, Normack's eyes grew wide and a shiver cascaded down his powerful body. Ty turned to face Normack with something that looked like a horse's bridle in his hands.

"Normack, I know what you're thinking, but I don't have any other ideas. If you bite down on this end, I think I can keep from falling off by holding on to the other end. That is if you do not mind this in your grip."

Normack looked over at Torg, then back at Ty. "I would kill

any other creature that asked that. But you're my friend, and I'll do this once for you."

Ty held out his rope and Normack gently bit down on it just firm enough not to snap it in half.

"Wait, there's one more thing!"

"If you're planning to make a saddle, the deal is off."

"No that's not it'" Ty realized that if he showed up in town riding on the back of a giant vipercon, it would mean real trouble for him and his family. So he used the last strip of his sweatshirt and made a mask to cover his face.

Ty was ready. He jumped up on Normack's back and held on tight. Then with the determination of a thousand dragons, he called back down to Torg. "I'm sorry, but there's not enough room up here for both of us. Try to keep up as best as you can."

"What do you mean?" boasted Torg with a sarcastic grin from ear to ear. "It's time you found out what a Zintarian warrior is truly made of. I just hope you two can keep up with me! Now let's make some serious tracks."

Torg flung his bow behind his back and lowered his head. With a flick of his tail, he disappeared in a flash.

Ty looked down at Normack and started to laugh. "I didn't think that guy could move that fast. But he had better watch his back because here comes one vipercon on a mission. Okay, Normack, I'm ready. Let's finish this!"

Ty held on to that rope for dear life as Normack slithered through the forest like a freight train dancing to music.

"C'mon on, Normack, what are you waiting for? Go faster! You've gotta go faster," Ty screamed.

"I can't! If I go any faster, you'll die if you fall off."

"If we don't catch up to that thing in time, there'll be nothing left for me to live for. It's all or nothing now, don't hold back!"

"Then may the winds of luck be with us. Hold on Ty, hold on tight! Whatever you do, don't let go, or there'll be nothing left of you to bring back to your village."

Ty let out a thunderous roar, ducked down low, and clamped down on those ropes with an iron grip.

Normack took off like a shark in blood-filled water, slashing his way through the trees and over anything that lied in front of him. The wind was whipping through Ty's hair so hard he thought it was going to get ripped right out of his head.

"I still can't see him, Normack. How much farther could he be?"

"I don't know, but his scent is getting stronger, and that can only mean that we must be getting closer."

The trail turned to a blur as the trees and bushes that lined the path looked like a green smudge smeared across the rocky mountainside. Determined to get a better look, Ty let go of one hand and stood up on Normack's back. He could hear the chilling sound of trees slamming to the ground by that rinog's rampage echoing through the forest in the distance.

"We're getting closer, Normack. I can hear him," shouted Ty.

"Get down before you kill yourself!" snapped Normack. "We're almost out of the Shadow Forest, just a little farther."

Seconds later, Normack burst out of the forest and into a huge green meadow. Ty almost fell off when he saw the rinog's trail heading straight for his village. He was hoping Normack was wrong about what he saw, but there was no doubt about it. He could clearly see where the rinog was heading.

"Look over there, Normack. There he is!" yelled Ty. "I can see him. He's headed straight for the razor bushes. Normack, we have to hurry. I doubt if those bushes will stop him. He's crushed everything else in his path so far."

As that monster was getting closer and closer to the barricade of razor bushes, Normack noticed a small cloud of dust coming up from the trail just up ahead.

Ty started to laugh and smacked Normack on his side, "Would you look at that, Normack? Just over that hill, I think it's Torg. Man, that guy can really move."

"Yeah I see him, and he almost caught up to the rinog."

"Be careful, Torg," shouted Ty as loud as he could. "Don't get too close to those bushes."

However, they were still too far away for Torg to hear them; all they could do was watch.

In just moments, Torg was close enough to make his move.

He dove straight at the rinog with his dagger in hand. But that rinog must have heard Torg getting closer because as soon as he lunged, it spun around and smashed Torg right in the jaw.

Torg flew twenty-five feet back and landed in a row of tiger cactuses. Their thorns dug in deep, scratching him across his face and down his back.

"You'll pay dearly for that," hissed Normack in a thunderous voice. "I promise you. Hey, Torg, we're coming. Just hold on."

Still too far away to help, they could only watch in horror as it pounded its chest and walk over to where Torg was lying. They could see the fire in its eyes as it stood there panting and growling like a mad dog. But just as it looked like it was going to walk away, it reached down and picked up a boulder and raised it high over its head. Torg had no chance at all; he was at the mercy of that giant, and rinogs never show mercy.

"Don't even think about it," screamed Ty in a voice that exploded across the field.

The rinog turned around and saw Normack approaching fast, with Ty standing tall on his back. With a snort, it turned and let out a roar so mighty the grass in the fields blew down as if a wicked wind was sent by the devil himself. It threw that boulder straight at them, but Normack was too fast as it slammed into the ground, crushing the field flat just inches away.

"You're gonna have to do better than that, scum bucket," shouted Ty.

It let out another earthshaking roar and headed off toward town. But when Normack finally made it to where Torg was lying, the creature was gone.

"Are you all right?" screamed Ty, jumping off Normack's back, prying the bushes free with his bare hands.

Torg slowly opened his eyes and looked around. "Did I get him?"

"Almost," laughed Ty. "If it weren't for us making so much noise, you would've gotten him."

As soon as Torg sat up, they heard a gruesome sound that can only be described as a thousand knives slicing through flesh. That's when they saw the rinog blasting right through the razor bush barricade as if it was a pile of leaves. Nothing was going to stop it now, as it headed straight for Ty's school.

"Are you all right, my friend?" Normack asked softly while he tried to smash down the rest of the bushes.

"Yeah, I'll be alright," Torg mumbled, rubbing his head. "The only thing that hurts is my pride and maybe my jaw a little bit."

"Hey, Torg," smirked Ty as he helped him to his feet, "that was the second time that thing busted you in the chops. If you don't start blocking those hits, he's going to rip your head off."

"Whatever! I'm just wearing him down!"

Ty stood up and stopped Torg from going any farther. There were so many jagged pieces of razor bushes lying around that they would be sliced to ribbons if they got any closer.

"Well, what are we waiting for?" shouted Normack as he coiled around them. "Jump up, and let's get going."

Ty didn't hesitate for a second; he jumped right on Normack's back, then leaned over and helped Torg up. After a few quick swishes of Normack's massive tail, they arrived in front of the hedge, and Normack started to slither over. You could hear the screeching sounds of the razor bushes scraping and slicing Normack's belly as he slipped past the barricade and into the outskirts of Ty's village.

You could see the path of destruction that led straight for the school. Twisted pieces of bikes and shredded books were scattered everywhere. The swing set Ty loved to play on with his brother was turned into a pile of twisted metal. There wasn't much left of the playground after that rinog ran through it. The sound of kids screaming and crying was filling the air.

Ty, Normack, and Torg prayed that they weren't too late and nobody was hurt.

"Help those kids," ordered Ty as he leaped off of Normack's back. "Keep them safe inside the school. That's more important than anything. I'm counting on you, Torg."

Torg didn't question him at all. He leaped down and headed

straight for the school.

"Don't worry. I will. You can count on me."

Just then, three of Ty's teachers came rushing out of the side of the school, armed with brooms and bats, ready to fight. When they got a look at Ty standing on the back of a vipercon with his armor shining in the bright sunlight and holding his sword, they stopped dead in their tracks. With their mouths hanging open, they couldn't believe what they saw.

"Get back inside the school and lock the doors. My friend Torg will protect you and stand guard."

After they ran back inside, Torg kicked the door closed, then used the bike racks and the chains from the busted-up swing set to barricade the doors tight. In moments, the school was secure. Smiling at a job well-done, he climbed straight up the wall of the school and waved at Ty to tell him everything was all right.

As soon as Ty got the signal, he looked around to find out where that rinog was now.

"There he goes," shouted Normack. "It's headed right down the street."

"I don't believe it. That's my street over there,'" screamed Ty. "That thing is headed right for my house!"

"He's too far away," shouted Normack. "We'll never catch up to him in time."

"I've got it," Ty screamed as he ran to the edge of his baseball field. "Normack, come over here quick, and grab the top of that tree and pull it down, all the way to the ground. Hurry, you got to do it now."

Normack coiled up, and as fast as lightning, he snatched the very top of that great tree. Then with all of his might, he started to pull. You could hear that tree pop and creak as Normack used his incredible strength to pull it down. It must have been the hardest thing he had ever done in his life because Normack had to wrap his tail around another tree just to anchor himself down. After two more tugs, that tree's top was lying on the ground by Ty's feet.

"You did it! Thanks Normack. I'll see you when the battle' over," shouted Ty as he jumped on top of the tree, and with one slice, he chopped it loose from Normack's grip.

Ty shot into the air like a bolt of lightning. He was determined there was nothing in this world that would stand in his way. He finally realized that he always had the power to do what he knew was right, and nothing could ever take that from him. He remembered how scared he was the first time he saw a rinog. But the only thing he wanted now was to wrap his hands around its throat. It was time to make things right again, and that rinog wasn't going to stop him.

CHAPTER 12
THE BATTLE OF ALL BATTLES

Ty could see the people below in shock as they stared up at the sky, watching as he flew over their heads. All the men in town came running out of their homes after the rinog, armed with anything they could grab, but Ty knew they wouldn't stand a chance. It would be up to him.

"Stay inside!" Ty shouted, zipping over the trees. "Keep your families safe. This is my fight. I'll deal with that rinog myself."

As Ty flew closer, he saw the beast crossing the street in front of his house, heading right for his yard. The sound of popping and cracking burst up from below as his favorite climbing tree in his neighbor's yard slammed to the ground.

Ty grit his teeth, and with a thunderous voice, he roared out, "You've caused enough trouble around here and now I'm mad! I know a cool game. Wanna play?"

The rinog turned around, looked up at Ty, and let out a bone-chilling grunt as smoke shot out from its nostrils.

Ty held his shield tightly against his shoulder and tightened up every muscle in his body. "Tag, you're it!" Ty shouted out with the roar of a titan.

There was absolutely nothing that rinog could do except watch as Ty attacked with the fury of a thunderstorm, slamming into that monster with all his might.

Kaboom! The shock wave of that mighty blow rippled across the land like thunder. He hit him so hard the windows in his neighbor's house shattered, and it sent him flipping across the street and smashing into old man Grady's pool.

After Ty came to a skidding stop, he slowly stood up, shaking his head, trying to regain his senses after that incredible impact. "Where do you think you're going?" boasted Ty as he twirled his sword then pointed it right at its face. "You started this fight, and it's about time I finished it."

Ty raced across the street, heading straight for old man Grady's backyard. He jumped over the tree and darted around the back of the house just in time to see that rinog lying face-down in the washout sand and muck. Shards of twisted metal were scattered all across the yard while chunks of its blueliner went floating away in a rush of water down the street.

"Looks like that bath didn't cool your temper down at all," Ty shouted.

Watching closely as it slowly crawled to its feet, Ty braced himself for whatever that creature had in mind. It just stood there wobbly and dazed, like a bowling pin ready to fall. After standing there for a few seconds, it shook its head and let out a powerful snort. As its huge muscles began rippling in the soft sunlight, it lowered its head, gazing at Ty with a burning hatred. The dripping wet satchel, full of blue fire rubies, was still clenched tightly in its grip. There was no doubt about it. That rinog wanted to rip Ty's heart right out of his chest.

Oh yeah! It was on.

Ty stood there, bravely and confidently staring straight into the face of the gigantic beast. This monster must be at least ten feet tall. Its eyes glowed with anger, and every muscle in its body throbbed with hatred. But Ty just stood there defiantly with his shield held high and his sword held tightly by his side.

100 The Battle Of All Battles

Suddenly, old man Grady kicked his back door open with a kitchen knife in one hand and a fork in the other. "Look what you've done to my pool, you . . . you . . . you, what the heck are you?"

"Get back inside and lock your doors," shouted Ty. "He's mine!"

Then jumping onto that smashed tree stump, he roared like a lion in the forest. "You better drop my bag of blue fire rubies horn head and leave this place forever. Or I swear I'll kick your butt all the way back to the Shadow Forest."

With that, the rinog let out a growl that would have sent shivers down the spine of the devil himself.

"So what are you waiting for, you horn head? Are you afraid of a fair fight?"

That was all the rinog could take; it started to charge. The ground trembled as it ripped through the yard toward Ty, sending grass and mud flying in the air and slapping against old man Grady's house. You could see glimpses of Ty's neighbors peeking out of their hiding places, watching in shock and horror while Jace and Carson, two of the high school football players, snuck back and forth cautiously behind the trees, looking for an opportunity to attack. But Ty just stood his ground—strong, defiant, and alone. It was too late to rethink his plans or wait for Normack and Torg.

Ty patiently waited as it got closer and closer. It was as if nothing else existed; there were no sounds of birds in the trees or even the faint sounds of kids playing. The town was so still that even the soft warm breeze faded to nothing. All you could hear was the booming sound of the rinog's pounding steps crushing the ground as it charged.

With a hideous crash, they met in battle. Ty hit that rinog with all his strength, matching it blow for blow. His shield was blackened with dirt and mud as they rolled across the ground, pounding each other with everything they had. Then with a surprising move, Ty jumped on its back and wrapped his arms around the rinog's neck.

Its eyes bulged with shock and anger as it thrashed wildly, trying to knock Ty off. But after a few seconds, it realized that it couldn't shake him loose. So it looked for the biggest tree around and slammed into it so hard it ripped it right out of the ground and exploded its trunk into splinters.

Luckily, Ty saw what it was planning to do, and in a split second before that powerful impact, he let go and tumbled into a deep ditch.

"Missed me, horn head!" he shouted as he leaned against what was left of a fence.

But when the rinog turned around, he tore off a huge branch with a loud grunt and dove into that ditch, swinging wildly.

Clouds of dirt and grass shot out in every direction as it tried to pulverize Ty with that chunk of timber. But Ty was way too fast for him and hacked his way through that savage attack with his sword.

"It's not going to be that easy," shouted Ty. "You have no idea who you're messing with!"

In a flash, Ty sprung out of the ditch and spun around, smashing that beast with his sword in the back of its head and knocking it face-first into the mud again. A blow like that would have taken the head off of any other creature, but the rinog just shook it off.

Ty knew he had to get that beast away from the middle of town, so he figured he should head to the lake. That way, his village would be safe and he could finish the fight there.

As soon as that rinog stood back up, Ty jumped up and came crashing down on its head with a powerful blow again. Crack! This time, he hit it with his shield so hard that it nearly popped out of his grip.

"How did that feel?" smirked Ty as he started to grin. "Because if you want some more, you'll have to catch me."

Ty took off as fast as he could across old man Grady's backyard and down the street. Then as soon as he passed the old willow tree, he headed down the hidden trail he always took with his friends.

The rinog charged at Ty as fast as a six-legged fire rasp and started catching up fast. Fortunately, Ty knew that trail like the back of his hand; he knew where all the soft sandy ground was, and he led it straight into a murky sinkhole.

With a huge splash, it fell face-first into the biggest sinkhole in town. Chest deep and roaring with a thunderous vengeance, it thrashed wildly to get out of the deep pit, but it never let go of Ty's sack of blue fire rubies. All Ty could do was stand there and watch as it slowly made its way to the edge of the pit and climb back out. Frustrated that his trick didn't work, Ty took off for the lake again.

The rinog was so blinded by the desire to kill Ty, it got down on all fours and charged with a monstrous fury.

But Ty made it to the edge of the lake just a few steps ahead of the charging monster. With a quick move, he jumped onto a log, flipped over the rinog's back, and landed a tremendous blow with his sword. Smack!

"I'm right behind you, horn head," boasted Ty as he stood there with his arms crossed. "So drop the stuff and leave before you get hurt."

The beast didn't listen to a word Ty was saying. Its heart was full of hatred, and its eyes were blinded with rage. It continued its attack with a fury never seen before. It swung wildly as it tried to beat, smash, or crush Ty to death.

Ty jumped back into the water to avoid its savage attacks. Hit after hit, they tumbled and wrestled across the shore. The water began to explode with rage as the fight ripped through its waters. But the more they fought, the harder it attacked. Ty knew he couldn't take much more of this and decided he had to end it fast before the monster killed him. He knew his only chance to defeat it was to use all his skills and outwit it.

In a flash, he got an idea and turned back toward town, running straight for the great pit. But the rinog was standing a bit too close, and its reflexes were as sharp as a razor. Just like that, it reached down and snatched Ty off his feet. It finally had him right where it wanted him. Ty wiggled as hard as he could, but the rinog had him locked solidly around his waist with a crushing grip. The more he struggled, the tighter it squeezed. Ty looked all around, but Normack and Torg were nowhere around. He was all alone in its cold grip of death.

Ty started to get angrier and angrier. You could see the emotion starting to boil deep inside him like a blazing volcano, red with power and burning with passion. There was no more fear left in his eyes or panic in his heart. Ty was a warrior with the heart of a black dragon.

It was an amazing thing to watch as Ty's eyes started to turn red with the power of justice and the mighty strength of determination. The rinog kept squeezing as hard as he could, but Ty's armor held strong. That beast thought that it had Ty where it wanted him, but it was Ty that had the rinog just where he needed him.

Ty reached out with the strength of ten men and grabbed ahold of the rinog's horn with his left hand, then pulled it right up to his face and stared right into its glowing eyes. Its breath was burning hot and smelled like the sulfur that burned in the deepest pits of demon's cave.

Then with a voice that shook the graves of his ancestors, Ty roared out with a brazen command, "You've terrorized the people of Zintar, you have caused great devastation to the people and creatures of this valley, and you have stolen treasures from me. You are to drop that sack and leave here forever, or you'll die here today!"

The rinog let out a mighty roar and tried smashing down on Ty's head with all its strength. But Ty blocked every explosive punch with his shield, sending a shower of sparks flying in all directions.

Ty shook that great beast's head and then pulled it closely again. "Stop this now, or you'll leave me no choice!"

That's when the rinog spoke out for the first time in a voice that sounded like an earthquake ripping through the depths of the earth. "Who do you think you are to order me to do anything? I will crush your bones into dust and take whatever I want, whenever I want, and you'll never stop me."

Ty looked deep into its eyes and said boldly, "I am Cobasfang, Lord of the Shadow Forest. And you will obey me, or you'll regret being born!"

"You're Cobasfang?" it laughed wildly as a puff of smoke shot out from its nostrils. "Not only will I kill you, but I'm gonna kill everything that lives in this place just for fun."

Ty held his head up high and roared out like thunder, "I am Cobasfang from the Shadow Forest. I banish you from these meadows forever, and you will never trespass into the caves of the lost souls again." Then Ty held his sword high into the air, and as the light sparkled off its razor edge, he shouted, "You are banished!"

Then Ty slammed the hilt of his sword deep into the rinog's arm. It ripped right through its tough hide like butter and dug deep into its flesh. Its eyes sprung wide as the pain shot through its body like a bolt of lightning. Instantly it let out an earth-shattering howl that echoed across the land.

The rinog threw Ty and the sack of rubies across the beach and grabbed its arm with a blood-curdling scream, then fell to the ground, kicking and rolling in pain.

There must have been some venom left in Normack's fang Ty used for the hilt of his sword because the rinog's arm started to curl and twist, then turn black as coal.

Ty hopped up on that tree stump and pointed his sword right at its face, "Leave now and never return. I am protecting this land. If you ever return to this place again, I'll not show you mercy. You will be destroyed!"

With that, the rinog crawled back to his feet and ran along the edge of the lake, and disappeared back into the thick forest.

Then as soon as the ground stopped shaking, Ty collapsed on the beach and staring up into the bright blue sky. He was still a bit dizzy and hurting from head to toe, so he just laid there groaning in pain.

Suddenly, he heard the sound of soft footsteps approaching. When he turned his head to see who was coming, he got the surprise of his life. It was his little brother, Bob. He was so excited to see his brother he nearly jumped in the air, but he knew he couldn't let him find out who he was.

"Are you okay, mister?" Bob asked softly as he stood above Ty's head. "You don't look so good."

"Yeah, I'm fine," replied Ty in a deep whispery voice. "I am Cobasfang. I have a gift for your grandmother and all that live here in this village. You don't have to worry about that rinog ever coming back here again. Now take this sack of blue fire rubies to your Mom. She'll know what to do."

Ty tossed the rubies into Bob's red wagon and smiled. "Wait, there's one more thing." Ty drew his sword and cut the string to his pouch that was filled with jewels from around his waist. "Give this to your father. It is a gift from your brother, Ty. Tell him not to worry. Ty will be home soon, and he told me to tell you that he loves you."

Bob was so excited that he started running back home.

"Wait, you forgot your wagon," chuckled Ty as he rolled it over to him.

"Oh yeah, sorry," Bob replied as he stopped and looked back.

Ty got behind the wagon and helped push it through the sand until he made it to the street. Then waving goodbye, he stood there smiling as his brother headed home. The wheels of his wagon were still squeaking and wobbling as he turned the corner next to his uncle John's ice-cream store.

Ty sat down again with a smile on his face, then stabbed the ground with his sword and leaned on its bloody hilt. As he started to regain his strength, Normack and Torg came strolling over the hill and sat down next to him.

"It's good to see you again," said Normack as he slid up next to the stump. "Are you all right?"

"Yeah, I'll be okay. I don't think that rinog will ever bother this place or Zintar again."

Torg sat down next to Ty and gave him a nudge. "I saw that you gave the sack of blue fire rubies to that little boy a moment ago. Who was that?"

Ty just smiled and pointed down the street. "That was my brother, and everything's gonna be fine now. Except there's one little thing I've gotta get."

"What's that?" asked Torg.

"The ring Queen Lylah gave me must've fallen into the great pit, and I want it back!"

Normack leaned down and let out a sigh. "Looks to me like you can't hold on to anything very well. The last time you lost something, it nearly killed us all. Is that ring worth your life? That place stinks of cave rats. Don't you remember the last time you tangled with one?"

"Dang right I remember. You don't have to worry about me anymore. I mean, how much trouble can we possibly get into?"

Then he pulled his star crystal from his pocket and turned to Torg. "Would you do me a favor and tie this off somewhere real tight?" Then tossed Torg the end of his rope and dove headfirst down into the pit.

Torg couldn't believe what Ty just did, but he moved like lightning and tied the end around the big tree stump next to the pit.

"What in the world does that guy think he is doing, Normack?"

"Getting his ring back, I guess," laughed Normack as he went down the hole after him.

"You two guys are nuts," shouted Torg as he headed down the slippery walls of that great pit too.

CHAPTER 13
A DARK BEGINNING

The great pit was believed to be the most dangerous place in their village, filled with mystery and dark vicious creatures. Nobody had ever ventured to go down there before. That is, not until Ty dove in!

Ty sailed into the pit like a rocket, with Normack and Torg streaking right behind him. You could hear their voices echoing off the walls as they yelled and shouted with fearful excitement.

"Slow down," yelled Normack. "You're going too fast. That ring isn't going anywhere, and this ain't a race."

"Sure it is! The faster we get to the bottom, the quicker I'll get my ring back!"

As they traveled deeper and deeper, Ty's eyes sprung open wide as he let out a thunderous scream, "Oh no!" But it was too late. Crack! Ty reached the end of his rope and spun out of control like a top on the end of a string.

"Hold on, Ty! We're right behind you," hissed Normack as

loud as he could.

"Oh, man, I'm getting dizzy!" hollered Ty as his rope started to slip, and he fell a few more feet. "Hey Torg, it looks like the express ride from here on out."

"What do you mean?" Torg screeched as he clawed his way down. "What are you doing? Hey, stop that! Are you nuts? You're going to kill yourself!"

Ty didn't care at all; he just held his star crystal over his head, then cut the end of the rope with his sword. "Last one down is a rotten egg," echoed off the slimy walls as Ty disappeared into the darkness.

"Catch him, Normack, before he kills himself."

But Ty was too far ahead of them when he sliced that rope. In seconds, he started making out the faint shadows of the bottom of the pit getting closer. In a flash, Ty remembered the last time he fell down a deep hole, and he wasn't going to hit bottom like that again. So just as he was going to splatter on the ground, he pulled out his knife and stabbed it deep into the heart of the great pit's wall. Then holding on as tight as he could, he started slicing a long gash into its side. The sound of stone grinding on stone rippled down the cavern as he slowed himself down just enough to make it to the bottom safely.

"Nice move!" shouted Normack. "But if you try a stunt like that again, I'll kill you myself!"

"This is nasty! Hey, Torg, I thought this place would be like all the other places we've been in. But this place is covered in trash. It's like people were throwing their filthy garbage down this pit for years. It's gonna be impossible to find my ring in all this crud!"

"Don't worry. We'll help you, no matter how long it takes."

As soon as Normack and Torg landed in that heap of trash, they started to rummage around in the nasty pile of junk. There were old bottles, rotting chunks of food, and old rusty cans scattered everywhere. There was even an old rusty bike with little flower stickers on its crooked handlebars smashed against the rocks.

The more they searched, the more impossible it seemed they would ever find that ring. But Ty wasn't about to give up so quickly. He tore into that mess and searched as hard as he could.

Finally, after what seemed like hours of digging and scooping through clumps of nasty crud, Torg popped up out of a small pile of clothes and started jumping up and down like a little kid. "I got it, I got it. Hey Ty, who's the man? C'mon, say it. Who's the man?"

"Did you really find it? Dude, you're the man!" Ty was so excited that he almost fell on his face as he made his way over to Torg. But as soon as he got close enough to see Torg's face, he busted out laughing.

You see, while Torg was jumping around holding Ty's ring up in the air, he never noticed that he was covered from head to toe with old women's clothes. He had a yellow dress wrapped around his waist and a pink scarf hanging over his shoulder. Ty and Normack started rolling with laughter.

While Torg struggled to unwrap the scarf from around his neck, Ty and Normack suddenly stopped laughing, and their smiles quickly disappeared. The look on Ty's face began to fill with anger as he watched Torg throw the rag to the ground. Before Normack could make a sound, Ty reached down, grabbed his knife, and threw it right at Torg's head. His knife whizzed through the air and missed Torg's ear by a whisper as he dove out of the way.

"Are you crazy?" shouted Torg.

The chilling sound of a solid thud echoed across the cave floor as Ty's knife stuck right into the chest of a huge cave rat lurking in the shadows. Then smooth as silk, Ty grabbed his bow and sent two arrows whistling across the cave and into that filthy rat just as it lunged to attack.

An eerie squeal ricocheted down the cold black tunnels as it fell by Torg's feet. Twitching and snapping its sharp yellow teeth, it lunged one last time at Torg's throat. This time, Torg was ready; he swung around and kicked it as hard as he could, sending it crashing onto that small bike in the corner. As its tail slowly thumped to the ground, Torg turned and muttered back to them, "I think we're in serious trouble."

Normack rushed over and stood tall above it, his fangs glistening in the light of Ty's star crystal. "I told you it was too dangerous down here. This place is covered with trash and a perfect feeding ground. There must be thousands of these beasts everywhere."

"I know. I know you did. But we're here now, and there's nothing I can do about it. Look, guys, the walls of this pit are way too muddy to climb up. We've got no other choice but to head deeper underground and go through these rat tunnels. I'm sure one of them will lead to back to the surface!"

Normack looked over at Ty and flicked his tongue. "You sure do know how to get into trouble, don't you? Except this time, we're all trapped in a twisted maze of tunnels that are infested with deadly cave rats."

Ty just smiled and chuckled a little bit. "What are you worried about, Normack? We're gonna be just fine. I've got the perfect plan. I think we should head into the cave over there next to Torg because it looks big enough for your big fat head to fit through, and it looks like it might lead back into the Shadow Forest. You know, Normack, while you were taking a nap, Torg and I ran into a few of these cave rats in the tunnels by the Crystal Mountain. So if we're lucky, we might be able to make our way back there and get out."

Torg shook his head in disbelief. "You must be crazy! If we head back in that direction, we're gonna end up back at the caves of the lost souls. Don't you remember what happened back there? What do you think is going to happen if we run into another Norgon hunting party? I don't think we'll be able to hide with a fifty-foot vipercon by our side! I think that rinog hit you in the head too hard."

By the look on Normack's face, you could tell he had no idea what Torg was talking about. So Torg filled him in on the dangers that lay ahead if they should meet up with a pack of Norgon warriors.

Normack started gritting his teeth and flicking his tail sharply back and forth. "Tell me, little one. Was that ring of yours worth the danger you put us all in?"

Ty got so upset that he picked up a stone and shattered it against the wall, then walked right up to Normack and got in his face. "I didn't ask you to follow me down here, and I never meant to put you in any danger. I know that I can't climb back up that slippery pit wall, but I'm sure that you and Torg can. So you guys can take off right now if you want!"

Normack shook his head and then took a deep breath to calm down. "We're not gonna leave you down here on your own you fish feet! All we're saying is that you have to start thinking things through. Did it even cross your mind that diving headfirst into this pit might not be such a bright idea? Or how about challenging Grog to a fistfight? And oh yeah, let's not forget that bright idea of yours to fight a rinog all by yourself. Don't you see? You have to start making better decisions before it gets you killed. We're a team, and we're going with you, but you got to start using that head of yours."

Ty walked over to the dead rat, stepped on its head, and pried his knife and arrows free. "You're right, Normack. I'm sorry I wasn't thinking. I just wanted to get my ring back. I guess I have a lot to learn about this Cobasfang stuff. Thanks for sticking with me."

Now all three of them understood the dangers that could be lurking in the shadows ahead, but they made up their minds they were going to face them together. Normack, Ty, and Torg had proven themselves to be strong and valiant warriors. Still, the treacherous journey that awaited them would put their friendship and stamina to the ultimate test.

Just as they started to head down that cold and dark tunnel, they heard a strange slithering sound coming from right behind them. As they spun around, Torg spotted Ty's rope landing on the pile of trash.

"All right, I wanted my rope back! Someone up there must've seen it tied to that old tree stump and tossed it down! You see guys. Somebody up there is looking out for us. We'll be fine."

CHAPTER 14
THE FORBIDDEN LAND

Ty, Torg, and Normack all took a deep breath and started on their journey to find their way out. That long, deep pit sent them into the heart of the underworld. To make matters worse, the cave they chose was cold and damp, and the walls seemed alive with thousands of giant roaches scurrying up and down.

"This place gives me the creeps," mumbled Ty as he walked up next to Torg. "Have you ever seen so many dead roaches all over the ground like this before?"

"That's not dead roaches we're walking on. This whole place is littered with splintered pieces of bones and chewed-up skulls. That's the crunching sound you're hearing when we walk."

"Holy crap! You're right. Now I'm totally creeped out!"

Torg nodded with a reassuring smile, then turned and took the lead descending through the cave. Ty and Normack stayed back and watched silently as Torg cautiously cleared the way. With his tail flicking nervously back and forth, he headed out of sight.

But after just a few minutes he stopped, turned around, and waved back to Normack. "Pssst, Normack, come over here. Can you smell that? I don't like this. I can smell the moldy nests of a hundred cave rats. We must be getting close to their lair!"

Normack made his way to where Torg was crouched down, then flicked his tongue and thought for a moment. "You're right. I can taste their young in the air. The scent is coming from these cracks in the wall. There must be another cave right next to us. Be on the lookout for any small openings that they can fit through."

"I will. Just be ready to get out fast if we're spotted."

Ty was getting nervous as he listened to their whispers drifting through the cave. So as soon as Torg turned and started to leave, he ran up to Normack and tapped him on his back. "I heard what you said. How big of an opening should we be looking out for?"

"Any opening large enough for them to fit their heads through. If their heads can fit, then they can squeeze through. So watch out for any opening that's small enough for you to squeeze through, but don't forget, their young can be just as dangerous when they attack as a pack. They can fit through an opening as small as your fist."

"Great, you mean they can come out from anywhere?"

"Yeah, now you got it."

Torg's tail slapped the ground with a pop as he turned quickly and stared at Normack. "Shhhh. Would you two be quiet? They don't need any help from you two. It's bad enough they can probably smell us, but those things have sharp hearing too!"

Normack and Ty just looked at each other and didn't say another word as they followed Torg deeper into the tunnel as the sounds of scurrying rats started to get louder. Chills ran down their spines as they crept through the darkness. No matter how hard they tried, the crackling sounds of each step they took seemed to call out to every cave rat for a mile. "Here comes lunch."

Torg took his time and scouted out the area ahead, making sure to point out every hidden entrance the rats could use to ambush them. Each time he passed a large opening, he looked around for anything he could use to seal it up. With rocks and pieces of bones, he silently jammed them into the crooked gaps. He knew it wouldn't last long, but it might give them enough time to escape if they tried to come through.

As they sneaked through the tunnel and deeper into the earth, the floor became less covered with bones, and the stench of the cave rat nests began to fade away.

"We must be getting out of their nesting grounds," whispered Torg. "The air is getting fresher, and the ground is becoming cool and dry again."

Normack made his way back to Torg again and flicked his tongue a few more times. "I think you're right. I don't see any sign of them now. But I don't get it. Why wouldn't they come down here?"

"I don't know. This place is perfect for cave rats. It doesn't make any sense. Now, where's Ty?"

As they turned around, they saw him gazing at the wall with one hand on his hip and scratching his head. "Hey, Torg, what's this stuff on the walls over here? It looks like someone smeared wiggling green lightning bug guts all over it."

Torg stopped and walked back to where he was and looked very closely. "I'm not sure what that stuff is. Just stay away from it. It could be poisonous! Now c'mon, let's go."

"Hey, Torg, at least it doesn't stink like Normack's breath. This stuff smells good. It almost smells like honey."

"I said leave it alone!" snapped Torg as he walked past Normack. "I said, let's go!"

However, Ty just couldn't leave well enough alone. He wanted to check it out so badly that he grabbed his knife and sliced a small clump of tree roots out of the way so he could get a better look. But as soon as he started to slice into that slime, it began to wiggle around, then it sucked back inside the wall in a flash.

"Did you see that? That stuff zipped into the wall like it was alive!"

As Normack and Torg turned to see what Ty was talking about, the ground started to rumble and shake.

"What did you do now!" shouted Normack. "What part of leave it alone didn't you understand?"

"It wasn't me. I didn't do anything!"

The glowing green slime on the walls started to boil and erupt in a blistering frenzy. Everybody dove for the ground as pieces of thick chunks of slime spewed out from every crack.

"We've got to get out of here right now!" shouted Normack. "Follow me, you two. There's a cavern up ahead!" Normack didn't waste a second as he spun around and slithered as fast as he could across the ground like a wave.

"We're right behind you. C'mon, Torg, this stuff's like glue. Hurry up and grab my hand!"

Just as Torg reached up to grab Ty's hand, a sharp blast exploded right behind them, sending a large chunk of the wall smashing into Ty's back with a bone-crushing smack, sending him flipping across the cave headfirst into a crystal pillar next to a large puddle of goop.

Torg watched in shock as Ty's body slammed into that pillar and collapsed to the ground like a dead rat. "I'm coming, Ty!" shouted Torg as he sprung up and headed for him. Trying desperately to avoid the puddles of slime boiling up from the ground, Torg took to the air and clawed his way straight up the steep walls and pounced between the sharp and jagged pillars as the sludge slowly covered the floor.

"Stop playing around!" Normack shouted as a bubbling wave swept away Torg's only safe spot to land.

With nowhere left to go, Torg pried a large crystal free from the side of the wall and sent it slamming into the ground just inches from Ty. The horrendous thud echoed like thunder as the wave splashed against its side.

"I've got you now!" hollered Torg as he sprung down from the side of that cave while puffs of stone dust smoked off his claws as he sailed through the damp air.

With the grace of a spirit cat, Torg landed on that chunk of crystal and dug his claws in deep. "It's time to go, little one," whispered Torg as he gently rolled Ty over and sat him against the pillar. "Are you battle-ready?"

Ty slowly opened his eyes up and rubbed his head as he spit some blood on the ground. "Yeah, that thing hits like a rinog!"

"Then let's get out of here!" Torg shouted as he helped him to his feet. "This place is caving in!"

"Okay, Bob, let's go home. Dylan said we're going fishing after dinner, and I've got some homework to do," muttered Ty as he staggered to his feet.

"What did you say?"

Ty turned towards Torg with a little smirk on his face as he passed out and fell into his arms.

"Normack, Ty's hurt! I'll get you out of here, buddy. Just hang on." Torg reached down and snatched him off the ground, then slung him over his shoulder like a cold sack of dirt and bolted for the exit.

His long sharp talons gouged into the hard stone floor as he ran for his life.

"Run faster! Move those tiny feet of yours!" Hissed Normack as loud as he could.

"Shut up. I'm coming as fast as I can, you bigmouthed legless lizard!"

Torg tried as hard as he could to stay out of that green slime as it bubbled up from the splintered floor, but the air became thick and hard to breathe as that sweet and overpowering smell filled the cavern. Torg was getting dizzy and weaker every step he took as his lungs began to collapse. That sweet smell was a powerful poisonous gas, and it was killing him quick.

Normack swayed back and forth nervously as he watched Torg start to stumble and struggle as he carried Ty over his shoulder. He knew they were out of time, and he couldn't wait any longer. So he bolted out of the safety of that cavern and headed straight for them. But before he could get there, that bubbling slime already had them surrounded, and it was quickly closing in. Normack watched in horror as Torg staggered one last time and started to fall into the slime.

Then with a thunderous growl, Normack rose up and struck like lightning and snatched Torg and Ty around their waist. Trying with all his might to keep his fangs from slicing through their tender bodies, he bit down as hard as he could. Using the last bit of strength he had left, Normack picked them up and bolted towards the cavern.

He knew he had to move fast if he was to make his way to the cavern ahead. But with Ty and Torg safely clamped down in his grasp, it was hard to move as he stretched across the jagged rocks and razor-sharp crystals as the cave quickly filled up beneath him. With a sudden desperate lunge, Normack shot across the top of a boulder as it fell into the muck, blocking the flow of slime as he swept safely into the cavern.

Instantly, Normack coiled up as he set them down as gently as he could, far away from the fumes of that bubbling death trap. "Wake up, you two. Take a deep breath of this fresh air!"

Ty slowly opened his eyes and started coughing and gagging up what was left of the poisonous fumes. "What in the world was that stuff?"

"I don't know. But if it wasn't for Torg, you would've never made it out of there alive!"

Ty sat there for a moment, trying to make sense of what just happened, then rolled over and saw Torg lying on the ground next to him. After a few moments, his head started to clear and he reached back and gave Torg a gentle nudge across his shoulders.

"Hey, buddy, are you all right? Wake up. You're safe now."

Torg rolled his head around and looked over at Ty and started to cough up the poisonous gas. He lay there on his side, hacking and spitting out green chunks as he struggled to breathe again.

"No wonder there were no cave rats around, Normack," coughed Torg. "That place was a living death trap!"

Normack looked around and shook his head. "There's one more thing we have to consider. With all that shouting and all that noise, every creature down here knows exactly where we are. So I guess we don't have to whisper anymore."

"Now that's the spirit!" laughed Ty as he tried to smile a bit. "I never did like sneaking around anyway. I would rather walk down these caverns and make those creatures hide from us than us hiding from them!"

Normack lowered his head and slid right up to Ty. "I would like to agree with you, but whoever said cave rats would ever hide from anything lied to you."

"Look, you two, cave rats aren't the only thing we have to worry about," mumbled Torg while slowly sitting up. "Don't forget where we are. We have to keep a sharp eye out for Norgons too. We were lucky to make it out alive the last time we ran into a pack of those demons, and now our only escape route is blocked by that goop over there. We better play it smart if we are going to make it out of this one!"

Ty and Normack knew he was right, and after all that commotion, they knew if there were any Norgons around, they had to get out of there fast before they had company.

Ty reached over and helped Torg to his feet. "You're right again. We better get out of here fast. How do you feel? Can you make it?"

"Don't worry about me. I'm fit for battle, and I've got a pretty good idea which way to go. I'll take the lead, and if I come up to a split in the cave, I'll mark which way I went by scratching an arrow on the ceiling with my sword. No one will ever think of looking up there for my trail, so just remember to check the roof if we get separated."

"That's a real sneaky trick, Torg. Did Scales teach you that one?" chuckled Ty.

"No, that one I taught him," snickered Torg as he slapped Ty on his back.

Now Normack reluctantly shook his head, agreed to the plan, and then watched in silence as Torg walked off into the darkness.

"You're next, Normack."

"All right. Now remember, don't follow too closely. If we run into trouble, we'll need you to make sure nothing sneaks up from behind!"

Then with a strong whip of his tail, Normack slid off, skimming across the jagged rocks and disappearing in the blink of an eye.

Ty waited for a moment like Normack said, then picked up his star crystal and took a deep breath. He had a pounding headache from the terrible crash against that pillar, and his heart was beating with fear and excitement as he stood there staring into the blackness. "Well, I guess it's my turn," he murmured to himself as he turned and started down that cave behind his friends.

Ty walked cautiously at first, listening for any sign of danger. Torg's gentle footsteps and Normack's swooshing slither slowly disappeared behind the gentle sounds of water dripping in a haunting rhythm and filling the shallow murky puddles.

"Where in the world are those two?" Ty quietly thought to himself. The cave seemed to go on for miles, and the deeper he went, the harder the ground started to become. Torg's and Normack's tracks slowly disappeared as the dust faded away. He felt alone again; his body was aching and his fingers were getting numb from the cold damp air. Ty tried his best to keep his spirits up, but after he walked for about an hour, he came upon a large gash in the side of that cave that branched off into three directions.

As he looked around, he couldn't find a single track anywhere. There were no marks on the ceiling or carvings on the wall. He wasn't sure what direction they went. Ty held his star crystal as high as he could, pacing back and forth between each opening.

"Torg, Normack, where are you guys?" Ty whispered as loudly as he dared. "C'mon guys, which way do I go?"

But there was no answer at all. So he studied each opening as hard as he could, looking for the smallest sign that could help him find his friends. The more he looked, the more frustrated he became. He had to make a decision. He figured that he should try the widest path because Normack might not be able to fit through the other two if the walls started to close in.

Ty was mad and frustrated at himself that he had lost the trail of his friends, but he wasn't going to let that slow him down. So he drew his sword and slashed an arrow deep into the stone above. With no other choice and determined to find his friends, Ty boldly headed into that cave alone.

As he got farther into the depths of that cave, the walls seemed to get warmer, and he started to see small spiders and lizards scurrying around on the floor. Ty started to smile a little bit because he knew that if there were spiders and lizards around, then there had to be an opening around somewhere to the outside world. In fact, Ty got so excited he started walking even faster, looking all over for more clues to where an exit might be.

The air began to become fresher and cleaner. "I must be getting close," Ty muttered to himself. Soon, he started to feel a gentle, warm breeze. "There it is! I found a way out!" shouted Ty as he looked behind a stone wedged against the wall. The glistening sunlight was a welcome sight indeed. Ty pulled out his sword, pried the stone loose, and laughed out loud as it slammed to the ground with a loud thump.

As Ty looked around, he knew right away that Torg and Normack didn't come this way because there were no tracks in the powdery dust on the floor. So, he ran back as fast as he could to meet up with them so they could all get out of this place together.

Ty sprinted all the way back through the cave, jumping and hurtling over the boulders he had to sneak over just moments ago. When he got back to the cavern, he slid to a stop, then yelled out as loudly as he could. "Hey, you two, where are you guys? I found a way out!"

But there was no answer. His words just echoed into the darkness. So he took out his sword and sliced a big X on the side of that cave to mark the way out. Then with his heart pounding in his chest, Ty ran down the next opening after his friends. It only took a few minutes until he spotted Normack's smooth trail brushed against some moss on the floor.

"Normack, Torg, where are you guys?" he cautiously whispered. But again, his voice disappeared into the silence.

Ty started to get that uneasy feeling of danger lurking close by again, so he slowly drew his sword and raised his star crystal a little bit higher to get a better look at what was surrounding him. The only sound left in the cave was the sound of his heart beating softly in his chest.

After a deep breath, he slowly and silently crept deeper into the cavern until he spotted two huge boulders sprawled across the floor. They were hiding the entrance to an even larger cave below. So he ducked down, slid his star crystal back into his pouch, and crawled on his belly over to the boulders ahead.

Slowly, he peeked around the edge of the cold stone wall, only to see the broken remains of what must have been a great battle. Once Ty saw Torg's knife lying on the ground, covered with green blood still fresh on its blade, it only took a second to figure out what had happened.

CHAPTER 15
AGAINST ALL ODDS

A stone-cold silence fell over Ty's soul like a bitter wet blanket in a winter's rainstorm. There were shards of arrows and busted chunks of twisted chains scattered all across the ground. Ty climbed down the jagged cliff's wall and crept through the cavern, studying every mark and footprint on the ground. He found huge gouges gashed into the thick stone walls where axes hacked deep. There was a mighty battle here indeed, and by the marks left on the ground, he knew at least twenty Norgon warriors captured his friends.

Ty dropped his sword and fell to the ground in shock. He tried to hold back his tears as he looked around. He knew they should never have separated. They should have just stayed together because when they were together, they were invincible.

With tears in his eyes, he picked up Torg's knife that was lying in the slimy muck, wiped it off clean, and then tucked it in his belt loop.

There was a fire in his eyes that burned bright with anger as he stared down the lonely cave ahead. Those Norgon scums were going to be in the fight of their lives!

He started to take off, running down the trail left by the Norgons, then came to a skidding stop. He suddenly realized that if he wasn't careful, he would get himself captured too. So he thought for a moment and climbed back up the side of that steep and treacherous cliff wall and made his way down a narrow ledge, hiding in the cold dark shadows and lurking behind rocks. He had to be careful not to be seen or heard if he had any chance to rescue his friends. That is if they were still alive, and those monsters haven't had them for lunch yet.

The farther he traveled, the more he started to hear the faint sounds of clanging armor and stabbing footsteps beginning to drift through the air from the cavern below. The tracks he was following led him right into an underground Norgon fortress. Carved out of solid stone, its lifeless ground was littered with the bones of a thousand beasts. Ty crawled closer and closer until the choking black smoke from the torches on the walls below made his eyes burn and sting.

Ty sat back for a moment and wondered what to do next. He turned around and watched in fear as a troop of warriors marched through the iron gates. It was a struggle for him to stay any longer in that thick smoke, so he used a rag to cover his mouth to keep from gagging on the smoke and stench from rotting flesh that swirled up the high cavern walls.

"There's no way I'll ever sneak in there without being seen," he mumbled to himself. Then as the fear started to slowly slip away, his heart became full of courage as his body tensed with rage.

I don't know what crazy ideas went through Ty's head, but he stood up from behind the thick black boulder he was hiding behind. Then with a powerful leap, he jumped all the way down and landed solidly in front of the rusty iron gates of the Norgons' city!

With his shield by his side and his sword held high, Ty shouted out in a voice that sounded like the crack of thunder during a midnight storm, "I am Cobasfang! Lord of the Shadow Forest. You have two of my friends, and I command you to release them now!"

The tower guards didn't know what to do. They began scurrying back and forth, grabbing their weapons and slamming the doors behind them. Ty didn't have to wait long for his answer as a cloud of arrows filled the air, screaming a song of death as they headed straight for him!

Ty raised his shield, knelt on one knee, and braced himself as a wave of poison arrows and twisted spears slammed into his shield and stabbed the ground around him. Ty held his ground as hard as he could as their mighty attack smashed against his shield. But the ground was too soft, and he slowly started to slide back from the constant pounding from each hit he took. With the strength Ty had never felt before, he dug his feet in deeper and held his shoulder tighter to his shield. After the last arrow fell, he slowly stood up and lowered his shield to his side. "They're no warriors that can defeat me and no weapon that can conquer me! So let my friends go now, or I will tear this place to the ground!"

That was when he felt the ground starting to shake and rumble. Bursting out from the steel cages that lined the streets and dark alleys came twelve blood-covered cave rats, snarling and chomping their razor-sharp teeth. Each one was as big as a full-grown saber tooth jackal, with metal spikes on their collars and armor tied to their backs.

In a split second, Ty reached back, grabbed four arrows, and sent them all sailing through the air like rockets. They whistled through the iron gates and plunged deep into those charging monsters. Then as fast as he could, he fired four more and slammed them through the hearts of four more charging beasts as they rushed through the gates. But there were four left, and Ty didn't have enough time to fire another shot as they hopped over the rats still twitching on the ground and through the gates, charging at full speed!

With the strength of ten men, Ty bashed one with his shield and grabbed the second one by its tail; then spinning as fast as he could, Ty threw it across the courtyard and into an open window where a dozen Norgon warriors were hiding, ready to fire their arrows again!

You could hear their screams as a battle erupted inside the room. The sounds of smashing timbers crashed through the air as Ty watched one Norgon trying to crawl out of the window, only to be viciously dragged back inside again.

But Ty didn't have a second to waste as the two remaining rats ran through the tangled field of arrows wedged deep into the ground. The smaller one of the two was fast and nimble. It hopped and scurried through the maze and was about to pounce when Ty picked up a spear and ended its bloodthirsty attack.

Just as that beast hit the ground, the last vicious cave rat pounced. Ty dove out of the way as its teeth chomped down just inches from his throat. Then as Ty turned around and leaped to his feet, he drew his sword and sliced it in half, leaving its body quivering in a pool of its own blood.

With his muscles pulsing with courage, Ty turned around and faced the cold dark city again. He looked around, then lowered his shield and slid his sword back under his belt. A small bead of sweat dripped down his cheek as he stood there watching the hordes of Norgon warriors scurry in the shadows in their war-torn armor, clanging and rattling their swords in a fit of rage.

Just when he was sure that legions of warriors were going to charge out from every direction, a thunderous sound burst out from the darkness. The deep and ominous sound of a horn that could make the souls of one hundred dead warriors shiver in their graves. Instantly, the clatter stopped, and a silence fell over the area like a black mist.

Ty stood there watching as the streets became still and the city grew cold with silence. Then an old and bitter voice, crackling with anger, spoke out from deep within the shadows, "Who do you think you are to enter my domain? And why should I give you anything that my hunting party has captured?"

"I'm not going anywhere without my friends," Ty roared back. "If you want to live long enough to have your next meal, you better bring them back to me unharmed, or the next thing you'll find filling your belly will be my sword!"

"If you are speaking of that Zintarian scum and that pathetic snake, I will not release them. Zintarians are our enemies, and they all deserve to die! And for that other one, I plan to make that pathetic excuse for a vipercon my dinner tonight. Now if you don't wish to be my dessert, you should leave here right now!"

"You must be hard of hearing. I said I'm not leaving here without them. Hand them over now, or I'll rip this place apart!"

"Who do you think you're talking to, you puny man-child? I am Drockmar, War Lord of the Norgons. You are nothing but a foolish and scrawny young creature. However, I do enjoy a little sport before I eat, so if you accept my challenge of combat, no harm will come to you. If you survive, you and your pets will go free, but if you lose, I will roast you alive and place your empty skull on my wall!"

"How many of your pathetic guards do I have to kill in this challenge of yours?"

"All you have to do is defeat another stranger to my land, and I'll grant you your freedom."

"Sounds to me like I'll be doing you a favor! Now let me tell you something, Lord Dorckmar! If I do this and you don't keep your end of the bargain, I'll show you no mercy. You can count on that!" Ty shouted back with thunderous defiance.

"Then it is agreed! Now if you want some advice, I think you should hurry. Just follow the screams of your pets. That shouldn't be too difficult for you. I just ordered them to be chained together and thrown into the pit with the other outsider. I'm sure they'll be quite happy to see you!"

Ty walked cautiously past the open field between the wall of their fortress and the buildings surrounding the city. As soon as he was sure their archers couldn't get a clear shot, he bolted down the dimly lit black streets that were lined with torches made from the skulls of their victims. As Ty got deeper into that rancid city, he quickly realized that Lord Drockmar wasn't lying at all. It didn't take long until he could hear the faint screams of his friends echoing in the distance.

Frantically trying to find his friends, Ty's blood started to boil as he smashed his way through the barricaded doors that blocked the road into the heart of the city.

"Normack! Torg! Where are you?" shouted Ty as his screams for his friends bounced off the buildings and fell to the ground unanswered. Ty started to panic as he raced faster and faster with his star crystal clenched in his hand. There was no stopping him now. He didn't care about the dangers that lurked behind those closed doors anymore. Ty would fight an army if they stood in his way. As he closed in to the center of the city, the scratching sounds of claws against stone from the scurrying shadows began to rip his hope from his chest.

Soon, the sounds of cheering and screaming began filling the air; he knew he was getting close.

He stayed on that main road and headed toward the billowing smoke and flickering light coming from the crackling fires in the fields surrounding the ruins of a gigantic stone building. Its walls were covered with decaying moss, and large cracks ran up its ragged pillars. "This has to be the place," Ty thought to himself as he sprinted closer.

Just as soon as he got near, Ty spotted a massive section of its wall smashed to the ground and piles of rubble littering the streets in all directions. Ty started to grin because he knew he had found his way in. Without a second's hesitation, he shoved his star crystal into his pocket and burst across that open field with his shield in his hand and his sword held high. Dozens of Norgons, busy throwing chunks of twisted logs into the fires by its rusted iron gates, turned and screeched in panic as they scurried into the shattered cracks in the walls like cockroaches.

"That's right! You'd better hide!"

With an explosive burst of speed, he leaped onto the rubble and sprang to the top in a flash. The thunderous sound of thousands of Norgons' screeching cheers started to drive Ty into a rage. A roar of pure determination burst out as Ty soared into action. Jumping from shattered boulder to ragged stone, he entered the colossal arena. The cold walls were no match for his incredible sword as he hacked his way through the crumbling walls that blocked his way.

The sound of rock popping as it split apart echoed into the hallway as Ty kicked the last chunk out of his way. Ty stepped through the opening and stood there for a moment, then flipped his shield around. Looking across the empty hallway, he could see a small flicker of light coming from its far end, cold and full of hate. So Ty took off running as fast as he could as hordes of Norgons started crawling out from the rubble behind him. But he never looked back as he raced to the end of the hallway, then down the slippery steps into the arena. Full of anger and not a drop of fear, Ty swung his shield and smashed his way through crowds of scratching and scurrying Norgons to the great field cut deep into the ground.

"Get out of my way or I'll slice you in half!" roared Ty as he ran down the steps of that ancient arena. "Torg! Normack! I'm coming!"

Hundreds of Norgon started crawling over one another and scurrying up the walls, trying to flee as he ran through the crowd to the bottom row, then dove out of the stands onto the field below. With a tremendous thud, he hit the ground right next to his friends.

Rancid thick dust swirled all around as Ty stood there with his shield in his left hand and his sword in his right. Ty took one look around at that stadium full of screaming Norgons as they started chanting and fighting among themselves. With a grin on his face and without wasting another second, Ty spun around and sliced right through those chains that held his friends so tight.

"Get up right now you two and Torg; here's your knife back. I think you're gonna need it because I heard we're gonna have some company down here."

Torg crawled to his knees and pointed to the shadows. "I think you might be talking about him!"

Ty spun around strong and defiant with his sword held high, ready for a fight. That's when he spotted a huge figure lurking deep in the shadows. "Oh nuts, this is definitely not good!"

Normack shook the iron net off his back, then rose up high and strong. "Nice to see you again, fish feet. Do you have a plan? Or are you just winging it again?"

"I got a plan, Normack. And it's a . . . Well, we have to . . . I don't have time to explain it right now! I'll tell you later!"

Normack looked down and started to laugh. "You mean if we make it out alive, that's when you'll tell me what the plan is, right?"

"Yep, that sounds about right," Torg chuckled as he

brushed the dust off his shoulders. He's winging it again.

"Very funny, guys! We wouldn't be in this mess if you two didn't get yourselves caught!"

Torg walked over and stood by his side. "It doesn't matter how we got here. We're here now, and we're ready! So let's get this party started!"

With that, Ty turned and started to walk over to that figure lurking in the shadows. "Hey, I heard you got thrown down in here just like we did. So let's work together and get out of here. What do you say?"

All three of them just stood there silently, waiting for an answer as hordes of Norgons and clamored in harmony in the stands above.

But it didn't take long until they got their answer. Those beady red eyes glowing in the shadows slowly started to move into the light; Ty stepped back, then held his ground. He couldn't believe his eyes. "Crap, guys, I think we're in trouble!"

"What is it?" shouted Torg in his low rumbly voice as he strained to see what was coming out of those shadows.

"Hey, Normack, guess who!"

"What do you mean, guess who? What are you talking about? What do you see?"

Ty glanced back at Normack, slid his sword away, and pointed at the shadows. "Hey, Grog, it's been a long time. Hope you're not gonna hold a grudge about that little swim we had!"

Grog stood there for a moment and then started to tremble with anger. You could feel the air crackle with tension as he remembered their last encounter.

Ty turned to Normack and whispered over his shoulder, "That stink pit of a marsh must've been deeper than I thought."

Then with a deafening growl, Grog smashed the ground with his powerful hands and charged as fast as he could right at them!

Suddenly, a loud roar burst from the arena and echoed throughout the pit as thousands of Norgons screamed and cheered while they watched Grog's thunderous rampage.

"Looks like we have an audience," laughed Ty with his

hands resting firmly on his hips. "But this time, Grog isn't going to hurt us again!"

All three of them scattered as Grog charged in rage. They knew they were trapped and had no place to run. Ty grabbed his rope and tossed one end to Torg. "Grab the end and hold on tight. I have an idea, but you have to be as fast as lightning."

With a sinister grin on his face, Torg nodded his head. He was ready for whatever Ty had in mind.

Ty boldly stepped up and shouted out loudly, "Grog, we don't want to hurt you, but if it's a fight you want, just bring that boulder butt of yours right over here! Hey, Normack, here's my plan. When I yell now, I want you to grab Grog as tight as you can!"

"That's your plan? You're nuts! Don't you remember the last time we tried that?"

"Yeah, but this time I'm ready!"

Grog was furious and charged across the field like an avalanche.

"If this doesn't work, we won't have to worry about being someone's dinner! Because that thing is going to grind us into jelly!" shouted Torg. "We'll be a slurpy dessert!"

"Now that's the spirit!" shouted Ty as he smiled and picked up a big fistful of rancid dust, waiting to make his move. Just as Grog got close enough to pound him flat, he threw it in Grog's face and dove out of the way.

Grog roared out in agony as that stinging grit dug into his eyes. Thrashing his head and swinging his fists in every direction, he stumbled blindly past Ty and slammed headfirst into the wall.

The crowd screeched and clambered for safety as the great impact split the stands apart.

"Now that's gotta hurt!" giggled Normack as he slid around behind Grog.

"Yep, I do think old boulder butt has made a good impression!" snickered Ty.

Torg looked over at Ty and threw the rope on the ground. "Would you two stop playing? All you're doing is making it madder!"

"I know! That's part of my plan! We've got to get him so

mad that he'll want to smash us flat!"

"Well, it's working! At least he'll kill us quick!" Torg snapped back with his fists clenched like hammers.

As Grog slowly squirmed and peeled himself out of that wall, he started pounding it furiously with all his might. Huge chunks of stone and dust started raining down on the crowd while he smashed anything that couldn't escape. The sounds of Norgons squealing in terror filled the air as they scattered for their lives.

Then Grog turned and stared with stone-cold fury and ripped a huge section of that crumbling wall and sent it hurling across the field. Kaboom! A thunderous explosion ripped across the ground!

"Normack! Torg! Get ready!" shouted Ty as he ran to the middle of the arena. "I think it's working."

The rancid dust swirled across the ground like a storm cloud, then billowed across the stands. When it finally settled, Ty was standing with his shield in his grip and his head held high.

The crowd started to wail and cheer as Grog slung his arms out wide and roared like thunder. Then the ground started to tremble and shake again as Grog blindly charged with a glare of a thousand knives at Ty.

"Watch out, Ty!" screamed Torg as he watched Grog closing in.

"Get ready! Just a little closer. C'mon, Grog, let's see what you got!" Ty shouted with commanding determination.

Grog exploded across the field, sending shards of stone flying with each pounding step. In seconds, he was so close he could feel his steamy hot breath. There was nowhere left to run. Ty couldn't avoid his punishing attack. Their eyes were locked on each other; you could just see a small bead of sweat rolling down Ty's forehead as Grog drew back his fist and threw a horrendous punch.

"Now Normack, grab him now!" screamed Ty as he ducked behind his shield, taking a monstrous blow to the chest. Boom!

"No!" shouted Normack as he rocketed over and tackled Grog with a booming crash, then rolled across the ground in a furious fight. Clouds of dust and splintered bones swirled across the ground as Normack fought with every ounce of strength he had! Within a few seconds, Normack whipped around Grog and was able to get a crushing grip as they slammed into the steep walls of that terrifying pit.

"Now, Torg, let's get him!" shouted Ty as he jumped back to his feet.

The Norgons were screeching in shock and anger as they threw rocks and bricks down on them when they sprung into action.

"Hurry up. I can't hold him much longer! He's starting to get free!"

They dove right on top of their twisting and twirling bodies and went to work, tumbling across the ground.

Torg flipped and squirmed, then spun all around as he tried to wrap him up as tight as he could. With Ty pulling and tugging on the other end, they were able to tie Grog's hands tight to his chest.

"We got him, Normack! We got him real good!" screamed Ty as he cinched his rope tight. "You can let him go now!"

With a huge grin on his face, Normack slithered around and flicked Grog against the ground hard. "Now that felt good!" smiled Normack as he remembered the beating he took before.

Grog struggled furiously, rolling back and forth, as that rope dug in deep and strained under the intense pressure. But the more he struggled, the tighter it got. As the dust started to settle, the Norgons cheering stopped, and the three of them stood boldly next to Grog, exhausted and covered with bruises.

Torg bent over and spit out a couple of teeth, then turned to Ty and whispered, "We better find our way out of here right now! I don't know how much longer that rope of yours is going to last."

Normack and Ty both looked down at Grog and knew he was right.

Then suddenly, a voice echoed from the halls far above the field. It was Lord Drockmar.

"Well, puny little man-child, you put up a great fight. You've defeated that monster of stone. I'll allow you and your pets to leave here alive."

"Oh, great and powerful Lord Drockmar," came a simpering voice whispering from behind him. "Look there at the man-child. That little creature has the ring of Zintarian royalty! That one must not leave here alive!"

"You're right! Prepare the archers. That ring will be mine!" whispered Drockmar back to his minion.

"Puny little man-child!" Drockmar shouted once more. "Before I allow you to leave, you must return that ring to me! It's mine, and I want it back! Then you and your pets can leave, and you must take that thing with you! Now if you don't think that's fair, then, archers, get ready!"

Torg tensed up and nervously looked around as he watched the Norgon archers charge to the walls with their bows held ready.

Normack arched up, then slid cautiously by Torg's side and hissed in a nervous voice, "Did he just say take it with us?"

"Yeah, Normack, he did," he replied in disgust.

"Great! This day just keeps getting better and better!"

Ty stood boldly next to Grog, then lifted his sword in defiance. "This is my ring, and you'll never get your hands on it! Our deal was that you'd let us go if I defeated this creature! Now if one arrow falls to the ground, I swear to you, Lord Drockmar, I will cut this monster loose right now and let it rip this place apart!"

Torg looked over in shock, then muttered quietly, "Drockmar. Ty, did you just say Drockmar?"

"Yeah, he's the one that told me that he was going to kill you and Normack!"

"So he considers himself a Lord now?" Then he looked around to make sure no Norgon could hear him as he mumbled into Ty's ear, "Ty, listen to me! If that's Drockmar up there, he'll never let us go with Queen Lylah's ring still on your finger! He will kill us!"

"Then we have no choice!"

So Ty took a deep breath, then turned to Normack and softly whispered into his ear. You could see Normack's eyes grow with fright at what Ty was saying. "Normack, it's the only way," whispered Ty as he turned around and knelt next to Grog.

"Listen, I have a proposition for you. I could either leave you in this pit all tied up for eternity, or I could untie you and we could fight these things together! I promise if you help us, I'll even help you find your way back home! So what do you say? Do you want to stay here all tied up or not?"

Grog stopped thrashing back and forth on the ground and started looking around. You could tell he was thinking it over.

"Ty, you've finally lost your mind!" whispered Normack. "If you untie him, he'll crush us flat!"

"Untie him? Ty, did I hear Normack just say you're going to untie that thing? Are you two nuts?"

"Listen, you two, if we try to escape, we won't make it five feet before we're pin cushions! I think Grog would like it better to get back home than be stuck down here in this pit for the rest of his life. But if you have a better plan, please let's hear it."

Ty turned toward the balcony where Drockmar was standing and shouted back in defiance. "Now I know that you're a liar. But if I see one of your warriors anywhere around us as we leave or smell the stench of a single cave rat tracking us, I'll come back here and tear this city to the ground!"

With a smirk on his face, Ty reached into his pocket and pulled out a piece of diamond that was stuck in the corner. Then he pulled his ring off and threw the diamond chunk as hard as he could into the stands far above. Then with one last glance at Normack, he raised his sword and cut Grog free with a powerful slice.

"You're free. Now let's get out of here!"

Grog ripped the rope off from around his waist, looked down on Ty, and smashed his mighty hands together with a horrendous crack. Torg and Normack took a small step backward and looked over at Ty, shaking their heads and ready for Grog to attack. You could feel the crackle in the air as they hoped Ty knew what he was doing.

(To tell you the truth, I think Ty was making it up as he went along!)

CHAPTER 16
INTO THE DEPTHS OF EARTH

As the dust settled around their feet, the one question nobody had an answer for was how to get out of that arena alive. The walls were too steep for Normack and so slippery even Torg couldn't get a solid grip.

Ty looked over at Grog with a sneaky grin on his face. "Looks like the only way we can get you back to your homeland is if you bash these walls into dust. Are you ready?"

With a grunt and a twitch, he turned toward the wall that held them prisoners and then let out a deafening roar that ripped through that place like a bolt of lightning.

"Smash it to dust, Grog!" shouted Ty as he drew his sword and got ready for battle.

Grog ran over and started pounding with all his might. The shock waves that rippled through the ground began to make those tremendous stone pillars rock and sway. The cheering that once filled the arena turned into shrieks of fear as the sound of crashing bodies echoed across the field like a wave of terror. The crowd scurried for their lives as he pounded with all his might!

"Fire!" screamed Drockmar. "Kill them all!"

"Get back here, Torg!" shouted Ty as he reached out and snatched Torg off his feet by his tail and tossed him to the ground. "Stay behind me!"

Ty grabbed his shield and dropped to one knee. His muscles glistened by the light of the torches as he held his shield high and strong, preparing for the worst.

"I've got your back!" barked out Normack as he coiled up around those two, turning himself into a living wall.

As Drockmar's archers drew their bows and fired as fast as they could, Ty braced himself for the unrelenting barrage. Those poisonous arrows started raining down from every direction, splintering and shattering against Normack's thick scales and Ty's incredible shield. But as hard as they tried, they couldn't find their mark as the building started to crumble and collapse.

Grog's tremendous punches and fists of rage started to blast the thick stone wall into dust. But as soon as the last chunk of wall slapped the ground, he started pounding his way into the stands, thrashing wildly and sending the iron benches crashing into the scurrying crowds as he pounded his way out.

I guess even a rock monster like Grog looks forward to a little payback. Because as soon as he clobbered his way out of there, he charged down the first open street and started leveling everything in sight.

Normack raised his head over the rubble and destruction left behind, then looked back down. "I can't believe it. He did it! C'mon, guys, let's get out of here right now. The coast is clear!"

As soon as the archers loaded up for their next attack, the three of them bolted for the exit. Still under the cover of the thick dust swirling across the floor, they climbed out of there and stood in the dusty wake of Grog's rampage.

Normack looked around in disbelief. "This place looks like a herd of rinogs just ran through with their tails on fire!"

"You're not kidding, Normack!" replied Torg as he hopped

over the twisted remains on steel. "Now if we don't get moving, those Norgon creeps are going to regroup and attack. They don't run scared for long, you know!"

Everybody knew they had to get out of Norgon city as fast as they could and somehow find their way out of that underground maze. Unfortunately, the cave Ty found earlier was way too skinny for Grog to fit through. They had to find another way out fast, and they didn't waste any time discussing which way to go. They just took off running over the piles of rubble left behind by Grog's smashing rage and never looked back.

The thumping and scratching sounds of cave rats scurrying through the smashed buildings sent chills through their bones as they hurdled over the remains of the devastated building and the splattered carts scattered across the road.

Suddenly, the high-pitched sounds of arrows screaming through the air came rippling toward them again!

"Arrows!" shouted Torg as he looked over his shoulder. "Follow me!" Torg snatched Ty's arm, then turned and ducked inside the remains of a huge house with polished floors and golden drapes flowing down across its shattered windows.

Normack started to flick his tongue and taste the air around. "This place is empty. We're safe."

"What is this place?" Whispered Ty as he looked around at the polished walls and golden statues.

"I don't know," muttered Torg. "It looks like a king's palace in here!"

Suddenly, Torg spotted two ivory bows with golden strings perched high in a glass case above a stone wall.

"Check that out!" Torg shouted. "This must be Drockmar's place, and they must be Drockmar's royal bows up there! Now considering that thief stole my bow and threw me into a rotten pit to die, I think he owes me a new bow. So, I'm gonna take those two up there!"

Torg reached back and smashed that glass case with his fist, grabbed both of those bows, and grumbled, "Hey, Ty, since they're two of them, we both can have a new bow, compliments of Drockmar!"

"Nice! Don't mind if I do!" laughed Ty as he took the bow

from Torg and pulled back on its string to test its strength. "And grab a bunch of those arrows too. I'm about out anyway."

Normack spun around quickly and snapped at the both of them, "You two had better start moving it or we'll get captured again. But this time, I don't think we'll get so lucky!"

Torg and Ty jumped down and peeked through the curtains.

"Looks clear to me," whispered Torg as he closed the curtains slowly. "Are you guys ready?"

"Ready or not, we gotta go right now!" Normack hollered back, sliding towards the door.

With a sinister grin on his face, Ty ran back and hung his old bow up on the pegs of that shattered case, then slung the ivory bow over his shoulder. "I didn't want Lord Drockmar to think we're a bunch of thieves. So I hope he likes my trade," Ty snickered as he skipped towards the door.

"Stop messing around. Get out here," snapped Torg as he bolted out the door.

But when Ty was running out, he stopped when he spotted something sticking out from behind the curtain next to the door. "Check this out," he snickered to himself as he pulled a long spear out. "I've wanted a new one of these for a while." Then taking a deep breath, he grabbed something else, whipped the door closed, and took off down the street right behind Torg and Normack.

As they ran through the city, Torg spotted a few Norgons scurrying between the buildings and hiding behind giant mounds of trash. You could tell that they would attack in a second if they got half a chance. Their lifeless eyes seemed to glow in the dim torchlight as they watched from the safety of their hiding places. Even the giant vampire bats were flying in circles overhead as if they were waiting for the Norgon to give the signal to attack.

"This place is way too creepy," shouted Ty as he caught up to those two. "I'll be glad when we get out of here!"

"You're not kidding," replied Normack as he glided over a statue of a Norgon riding high on the back of a two-headed cave rat. "This place gives me the creeps too!"

Those three didn't waste any more time getting out of that place. They rocketed through the desolate streets like their tails were on fire until they caught up with Grog as he smashed through the last barricade at the edge of the city.

They kept up that swift pace, running for hours over bitter cold trails and slime-covered paths until the Norgon city disappeared into the darkness. The cavern became quiet again; even Grog's thunderous footsteps that echoed off the walls seemed to calm down into a peaceful drumming rhythm.

When Torg turned around and saw they weren't being chased, he stopped and shouted to everybody, "Hey, guys! Let's take a break for a minute. My feet hurt, and I think we all can use a little rest."

They were finally safe; the Norgons were nowhere to be found. They must have given up, or at least they were too afraid to show their faces. Who could blame them? The four of them together made a powerful army all by themselves.

Still, they had traveled deep inside the cave, and their muscles were aching with exhaustion. With a sigh of relief, everybody agreed and sat down side by side, hanging their feet over the edge of a deep crevice in the floor.

Grog, on the other hand, just leaned up against the cave's wall, exhausted.

Ty looked back and chuckled a bit. "Hey! Would you look at that? It's no wonder we never saw him that day in the field. He just looks like another part of the cave. That's cool!"

Normack just smiled and shook his head. "All he has to do is stay still and no one would ever know he was there!"

As Normack settled down, Ty gave him a sharp nudge in his side and started to grin. "Hey Torg, back in Drockmar's place, I found something you might like."

"Yeah, what's that?"

"I found this stashed in the corner. I thought you might like it back."

"Shear-Akon!" he shouted as he sprung to his feet. "I never thought I'd see my sword again. She was my father's sword, and he passed her down to me when he went to our ancestors."

"You're full of surprises. Thank you."

The three of them sat there for a while, smiling and tossing a few rocks down the hole, trying to see who could find the deepest part and betting one another that their next shot would be the best.

"This reminds me of back home," Ty muttered softly while thinking about his brother. "Me and Bob would just sit around and toss rocks down the great pit when we were bored and the fish weren't biting."

Torg looked over and gave him a little nudge. "I think I saw him back at the school, a kid was playing outside and he looked just like you."

"Hey, maybe. Bob was wearing a blue shirt, and I think he was wearing shorts. Was that him?"

"Shhhh," whispered Normack as he turned and flicked his tongue. "I think I heard something."

Everybody stopped and held their breath. The thought of the Norgons approaching made everyone expect the worst, and they started to prepare for battle!

"What is it?" whispered Ty. "I don't hear a thing!"

"It sounds like there's a river up ahead. I can hear rushing water coming from up ahead," Normack whispered as he motioned into the darkness. "There's always a way out of a cave if you follow where the water is going."

"Well, what are we waiting for?" Boasted Ty with a blaze in his eyes. "Hey Grog, get up. Normack heard something up ahead, and we think there might be a way out!"

It took a few moments, but Grog lumbered to his feet. Then with a low rumbling grunt, he joined the others trudging down that dark and narrow path.

Torg quietly lead the way through the treacherous cavern and trying his best not to slip on the slimy green moss growing thickly over the ground. The air was getting heavy and musty as they got closer to that underground river. The soothing sounds of the gentle stream flowing through the cavern sent the feeling of peace through our young warriors.

Finally, the cavern's walls began to spread out wider as they approached the river's edge. It was almost like the gentle arms of your mother as she welcomes you home from a long day. The cave was glistening with every color of the rainbow from the light coming from a split in the cave wall across the water.

"Great job, Normack! You did it! You found a way out," hollered Torg as he slapped him on his back.

"Let's try to cross over there," Ty said as he pointed downstream. "The water doesn't look too deep, and it seems to be calmer over there!"

"Are you sure you can make it across the river, fish feet?" snipped Normack kindly. "I remember the last time you tried to cross some water. It almost killed you. If you want, you can hold on to me and I'll help you across."

He knew Normack was trying to be nice, so he didn't get upset at all when Normack offered to help. However, the water looked shallow enough, and Ty knew he would be ok.

"Thanks anyway. I have to do this by myself. This water isn't deep at all. I'll be all right."

"I can't believe we're almost out of this underground maze," Normack shouted joyfully as he gave his tail a little wiggle. "I can't wait to feel the warm sun on my back again!"

Normack, Torg, and Grog splashed their way across to the other side pretty quickly, but Ty was still a little nervous, and he took his time crossing. He was in no hurry at all.

Then as soon Normack and Grog made it to shore, they headed out of the cave to bask in the bright sunlight. But Torg was just a few steps behind them, and as soon as he started to crawl out of the water, he looked over his shoulder at Ty—just in time to see something long and slithery swim up right behind him.

"Don't look now Ty. But you're not alone in that water. There's something in there with you! Get out quick!"

When Ty spun around, he was amazed to see a beautiful young girl with hair like golden silk swimming in circles around his legs. She seemed to be quite curious. I don't think that she's ever seen a boy before, or at least not a young boy with legs. She gently swam around Ty a few more times, then rolled over and smiled as if she was trying to say hello.

"Normack, get back in here! There's something in the water with Ty!"

Normack bolted back in and stopped on the distant

shoreline, trying as hard as he could to see what was going on. Torg looked kind of nervous because he knew the dangers that lurked in these dark waters. After a few more ripples swirled around Ty, Torg got his first look at what was under the water.

"Normack, whatever you do, just stay right there and don't make any sudden moves," whispered Torg as he held his hand out to stop him from diving in. "That thing swimming around Ty looks like a water witch!"

"What do you mean a water witch?"

"I'm not sure if it's a water witch or not. I hope I'm wrong because if that thing really is a water witch, Ty's in big trouble!"

"I'm not going to stand here and do nothing if he's in trouble!"

"Just listen for a second, you big idiot! Water witches are powerful sorceresses, and they'll trap your soul in the depths of the freezing waters if you make them mad! So just stay still!" he scolded as loud as he could and still not be noticed.

"There's nothing we can do to help. The only thing we can do is to wait for it to come out of the water, and when it does, I'll be ready," he whispered again.

The beautiful creature just stayed there, drifting back and forth in that crystal-clear water, looking deeply into Ty's eyes. Then with a soft and gentle smile, she reached up and touched Ty's hand as the cool water dripped from her fingers when she slowly rose up.

"Watch out, Ty, she is trying to cast a spell on you!" shouted Torg as he lowered his bow. Then with an earsplitting hiss, he sent an arrow straight for the heart of the witch.

"What are you doing?" screamed Ty! As he frantically dove in front of that poisonous arrow a split second before it hit that young creature. Crack! The impact of that arrow bounced off the cave's wall like a gunshot as it slammed into Ty's chest.

"What did you do?" screamed Normack. "You just shot Ty!"

Ty flew back and splashed into the cold dark waves of that unforgiving water and disappeared out of sight.

A hideous screech filled the air as the water witch spun around and saw Torg standing there with his bow in his hands. In a fit of rage, she exploded out of the water as lightning shot out of her fingertips.

The crackle of her powers burst across the cave, making the water boil and time stand still. Her eyes glowed with shock and anger as she stared at them, frozen solid by her spell.

Once they were firmly in her grasp, she reached down into the cold water and pulled Ty up, and held him gently in her arms as he started to cough up water and gasp for air. He looked into her eyes, and he could see her pain as she held him tightly in her arms.

"I'm okay," coughed Ty as he drew another breath. "My armor saved me from the arrow, and you saved me from drowning. Thank you!"

She let out a sigh of relief as a gentle smile crossed her lips while she slowly helped Ty to his feet. But her attention quickly snapped back to Torg and Normack, still frozen solid on the distant shore. Her rage grew stronger and stronger as the water surrounding her started to swirl once again.

"What are you doing? They're my friends. Please don't hurt them! They thought I was in danger!"

"They deserve to die!" she spoke out with an eerie voice. "They tried to kill me and they almost killed you. So why do you now risk your life to save them?"

"They were only trying to protect me! But I swear if you try to kill them, you'll have to kill me first!" shouted Ty as he reached for his sword.

She turned to Ty, grabbed him by his neck, and lifted him clear out of the water. "You are a strange young creature, willing to risk your life to protect me and then willing to die to protect them. Why do you risk your life so foolishly?"

"They were just wrong. They just didn't know any better," gasped Ty as he started kicking his legs. "Just like you right now! You're making a mistake. Nobody deserves to die because of a mistake!"

"Then why did you enter my domain if you weren't trying to kill me like the others?"

Ty kicked and struggled, then gasped for another breath.

"We weren't trying to hurt anything. We're just trying to escape from the Norgons! They captured my friends over there, and they were going to kill us. We were just trying to get away!"

The water witch looked stunned and surprised as she listened to Ty's words.

Then looking back at Normack and Torg, she nodded and gently put Ty back down and told him in a soothing soft whisper, "You are speaking the truth. I can see what you had done to free your friends in your thoughts, and you seek the Crystal Mountain."

"Yeah, that's what I've been trying to tell you!"

She stared into his eyes for a few seconds more than slowly slipped under the water.

Ty was memorized by her beauty and her kindness as he watched her hair drift gently in the water around him once more. But as soon as she swam in front of him, she slowly rose out of the water and gently spoke again. "Many have come before you and tried to steal my powers, but you are so different. You risked your life to save my life, and then you risked it again to save your friends. So I will grant you your wish. They will not be harmed, but they can never come back here ever again, for if they choose to return, I will not be so forgiving!"

Ty was so happy he started to giggle and reached out and gave her a great big hug. "Thank you! These are my friends, and I know they would never hurt anyone unless I was really in danger!"

She backed away, swirled around Ty once more, then stood tall in front of him. "Maybe they were right. Maybe I was thinking about keeping you for a while!" She laughed as she ran her fingers through his hair. "For your honesty, I will give you a gift. A gift to know when your friends are about to do something wrong. You will have the ability to hear the thoughts of those around you when your heart and mind are at peace."

"What do you mean? I'm not looking for anything. All I want is to get out of here before the Norgons come back!"

"If you do not accept my gift, then maybe I will just keep you for a while. Now remember this! Their thoughts will

145 Into The Depths Of Earth

come to you like a whisper in a dream but be warned. If you cannot control your anger, those voices will rage within you like a thousand screaming banshees!" she cackled as she rose up higher.

"Hey! All I want is to go back home with my friends!"

"But first, let me hold you!" she screeched out loud as she lunged forward and grabbed Ty's head with both hands. Her eyes turned black as she smiled and held him tightly.

"Let me go!" screamed Ty as he struggled to break free from her grasp. "I just wanna go home!"

A smile crossed her lips as sparks began to jump from her fingertips and slice through his body.

"Come to thee the sounds of silence!" she chanted as Ty's eyes started to roll to the back of his head. "Open your mind and catch the dream, winter's thoughts, and summer's screams! Into your mind, the thoughts will race, with a whisper and then with haste! Showers of night and into your dreams, birds of flight and raven's screams!"

Then in an instant, the still water turned bitter cold and started to crackle and freeze all around them as pillars of sparkling green ice shot up from the hidden depths beneath their feet. She smiled once more, then gave him a gentle kiss and laughed as he started to wake up from that trance.

"What did you do to me?" he muttered, half-frozen and confused.

"You'll see," she said with a sinister grin. "Or better yet, you'll know soon enough!"

Ty broke free from her grasp and ran for shore as the river burst into flames.

She spun around furiously once more, then smashed a pillar of ice with one strike of her hand. "Run, little one, run! But remember to listen with a still heart!"

The flames were as cold as a winter's night and felt like talons slashing across his chest. Then with a clap of her hands and a banshee's screech, she propelled Ty across the stream, and he landed by the feet of Torg and Normack, still motionless and covered in a thin layer of frost. You could hear her laughter fading into the darkness of the cavern as the water became calm again.

Moments later, Torg and Normack came out of her sick

and twisted spell. But when they looked down and saw Ty's frozen body lying by their feet, they gasped in fear.

CHAPTER 17
DARKNESS FALLS WITH DEATH NEARBY

Moments later, Ty woke up from his frozen slumber, staring up at Torg's and Normack's worried faces.

"Pick him up and let's get him into the sunlight where he can warm up," Normack said anxiously. "We have to get out of this place before that thing comes back!"

"Are you all right, Ty?" asked Torg nervously. "You're shivering so much I can hardly hold you up."

"I'll be alright. All I need is to get warm and find some willow bark. My head is pounding so hard I think it's going to explode!"

"Don't worry fish feet," whispered Normack as they walked out of the cave. "This warm sunshine will make you feel a lot better. Just lie down on this warm, smooth rock, and I'll stand guard and watch your back while Torg looks for some willow bark for your headache."

With that, Torg nodded and ran off into the woods as Normack made his way up the side of a steep hill next to the cave and kept a watchful eye for any sign of danger while he rested below.

"Hey, Normack! Where's Grog?" shouted Ty. "I don't see him anywhere!"

"I don't know! The last time I saw him, he was walking out of that cavern and heading down that hill when the water witch appeared."

"Water witch? What are you talking about?" Ty asked as he struggled to sit up a little bit. "Everything seems a little fuzzy. I remember making my way across that river when everything went dark. Then the next thing I know, I was waking up on the ground next to you guys, half-frozen. What in the world happened? And what do you mean about a water witch?"

Normack slid back down the hill and coiled up next to Ty. "Well, I don't know much about water witches, but Torg said he knew what she was right away. You see, when Torg spotted her swimming around you, he said she was some kind of wicked witch."

"Normack, did you see her?"

"Yeah, but not until we were onshore."

"Well, what happened then?"

"That's when he said he was going to scare her so you could have enough time to get away. But that's when things got really weird."

"Now it's going to get weird! This whole thing is weird. Was she some kind of mermaid or something?"

"Ty, I told you. I don't know what she was, but as soon as he shot his arrow, everything sort of stopped! We couldn't move, and we couldn't make a sound. It was like I was awake but still dreaming. Then the next thing I know, you were on the ground at our feet looking like a popsicle, and she was gone!

"Wow, I can't remember a thing. I'm just so cold, and I got the worst headache I've ever had!"

Normack moved closer to Ty to help him warm up, then looked back at the entrance of the cave. "I don't think it's a good idea to stick around here for very long! So as soon as you feel up to it, I suggest we get as far away from this place as we can!"

"You'll get no argument from me about that, rat breath,"

Ty snickered as he laid back down. "I wanna get as far away from here as I can too. There's something about this place that makes me feel really nervous."

"Well, which way do you think we should go now?" hissed Normack softly. "I got so turned around in those caves I have no idea how to get you back home!"

"I don't want to head back home right now," muttered Ty. "I want to help Torg find his way back home first. All he was supposed to do was to help me make it back home safely with those rubies. But it was my fault he followed me down that pit. So I guess it's my turn to see that he gets back safely this time."

Just then, Normack stood up and peered deeply into the woods. His muscles tightened and rippled beneath his scales. There was definitely something out there.

"I think Torg's coming back," Normack said in a low and reassuring voice. "I can hear some light footsteps approaching. I want to be sure first, so I'm gonna hide behind those bushes at the edge of the clearing, and if it's not Torg, I will deal with it myself. Just lie back down and warm yourself. I'll take care of it!"

Normack slithered silently across the deep green grass and disappeared into the thick brush as he hid and waited for whatever was approaching. It didn't take any time at all until a dark figure started to appear, quietly pushing its way through a tangled web of vines clinging to the trees at the edge of the pasture.

Normack made his move. He slithered fast and silently to head off the intruder before it got to where Ty was. But before that shadowy figure could slip through the wall of vines, Normack rose up tall and ferociously, his long ivory fangs sparkled in the evening sun, ready to strike.

"It's Torg!" shouted Ty. "Normack, wait! It's Torg!"

But Normack was too far to hear Ty's weak cry to warn him.

Torg pulled back the vines and jumped through a small opening he made. But just as he started to stand up, he was shocked to see Normack right in front of him, ready to strike.

"What are you doing?" barked Torg as he stuck his hand

in his face. "It's me, you big rat breath, snake in the grass, blind as a bat, idiot!"

Normack shook his head in disbelief. "What am I doing?" muttered Normack as he slithered back a few feet. "What in the world do you think you're doing running up through the brush like that? You were one flick of my tail from being my next meal. I've got half a mind to end this right here and now and teach you your last lesson in life, you little twerp. Never sneak up on a vipercon, especially me!"

"Sneaking? Who's sneaking? I was making more noise than a herd of glop stoppers in a forest full of dishes!" Torg screamed back.

"Hey, you two, stop all that yelling. I can't take it anymore. My head's pounding and I need some rest!" yelled Ty as he fell back against that smooth stone slab with a loud hollow thump.

They knew he was right, so they headed back to Ty without saying another word to each other. Except for a silent moment when they looked at each other and nodded as if to say they were sorry.

"You can relax now. I found a real old willow tree growing out from the edge of a cliff. I climbed all the way up to the top of that wobbly old tree and gathered as much sweet bark as I could. I hope this is enough," whispered Torg as he laid down a nice big pile of fresh bark next to Ty's side.

But Ty was so weak that he just smiled, reached over, laid his head on top of that soft pile of bark, and closed his weary eyes.

"Let's leave him be," whispered Normack. "He's too weak to move right now. He needs his rest and it's getting dark. Why don't you get some rest too, and I'll keep watch? Tomorrow's another day, and we're gonna need all the rest we can get if we plan to find our way out of this side of the Shadow Forest!"

"You're right. Let's all get some rest and start off fresh in the morning." Torg looked around and found himself a nice, cool, damp resting spot between two moss-covered boulders (just like the caverns he grew up in), then laid his head down and closed his eyes.

Normack slithered back into the tall green grass again,

happy to watch over them. However, this time he kept his watchful eyes focused sharply into the ever-growing darkness. He was the perfect one to stand watch in the dead of night. He didn't need a speck of light to know what lurked around, and with the slightest flick of his tongue, he could taste the air for any hint of trouble. He understood all too well that when nighttime crept into the shadow forest, the beasts that dwelled there came out into the cover of darkness to feed.

What made matters ten times worse was that they were still camped out at the mouth of the water witch's cavern. Even though the creatures kept their distance from this place in the light of day, in the dead of night, the evil that crept in the shadows were drawn to it with an unholy devotion.

There were no stars out that night, no sounds of crickets in the fields; only the passing dim glow that escaped from one of the twin moons slipped between the clouds before it was swallowed up by the cold night air.

With a relentless gaze, Normack stood watch over Ty as he tossed and turned on that cold, hard stone. Minutes seemed like hours while Normack's heart started to fill with fear as he listened to Ty moaning out in pain. Whatever happened to him in the waters of that cavern was ripping him apart. Normack feared that he would not make it through the night, and the only thing he could do was to make sure nothing else happened to him, no matter what.

Hours seemed like an eternity as he stayed still in the weeds. The sound of the tall grass swaying in the gentle breeze had an unnatural and spooky rhythm. It was the same creepy sound that filled the air just before something evil would show its face. It was way too quiet. Normack had that uneasy feeling that they weren't alone.

Torg must have felt it too. Because when Normack glanced over at him, he could see Torg's eyes slowly opening as he reached for his bow. With a questioning nod, Torg silently crept to his feet and slid around the boulders. "I'll go up to the top of the boulders." He motioned with the tip of his bow as he disappeared into the shadows above.

The fields were chillingly quiet; Torg could still hear the faint sounds of the river gently churning softly within the witch's cavern beneath him. As a royal Zintarian guard, Torg was bound to his oath to Queen Lylah to protect and defend Ty at all costs. But he didn't need to be reminded of the oath he took so long ago; he would gladly give his life to protect his friends. So he quietly slid out three arrows and gently placed them on the soft green moss by his side, then drew one more and readied his bow.

There they sat, prepared for a fight. The air seemed to tingle with danger as they strained into the darkness, looking, watching, and fearing for what might be coming.

Normack grew more impatient. He could feel the soft murmur of movement tickling his belly from somewhere, somewhere close. Still, he couldn't detect any trace of body heat or pick up on the scent of any creature creeping nearby as he flicked his tongue in the cool night air.

Suddenly, Torg stood up and drew his bow. "Over there!" he whispered to Normack. "There's something moving around behind that tree. It's getting closer!"

Normack ducked down and slid over to where Torg was gesturing. His scales tingled with the sensation of danger as he got closer. Just as he slid behind the small tree, something darted across Normack's back and dove back into the tall grass, but as soon as he spun around to attack, it was gone. Then another thing zipped past the tree, and as he frantically spun around again, there was nothing to strike at. It was gone. "Did you see that? What was it?" shouted Normack.

"I don't know. I can't see a thing. Wait . . . wait . . . there . . . Something moving over there." Torg fired his bow and sent an arrow screaming through the night. Whack! He hit his mark.

As Normack turned, ready to strike, his eyes filled with fear. "It's . . . its . . . wait! I don't believe it! It's a raptoid spider! Hey there, raptoids!" shouted Normack. "No wonder we didn't see anything. Those raptoids' bodies are as clear as glass, and they're totally invisible when they stand still. You can be sitting right next to one, and you'd never know it. So watch out!"

"The one you got was a young one. It's only about the size of your fist, and it's still wiggling around over here! That poison tip arrow you took from the Norgons has no effect on it."

"Are you kidding me? I know what they are! Those things are feared by everything that lives in the caves below. Even though their young may be as small as a pebble, their bite is ten times deadlier than yours! They can grow to be as large as a desert cat with fangs three inches long and can kill a full-grown rinog with a single bite!"

Normack took one more look at the grass in the field, swaying back and forth and shouted, "We got to get out of here now! The grass isn't moving because of the breeze. This field must be filled with thousands of those things, and the sun's coming up!"

"Well then, all we have to do is keep them back until they go back into the trees! You keep them back, and I'll shoot anything that gets by!"

"Torg, you don't understand! They can't survive in the sunlight, so they must be headed back to the cave, and Ty's lying right in their path. If they find him, they won't pass up a quick meal like that!"

"Hey, your scales are tough enough to protect you. But mine aren't, and Ty doesn't even have any. We gotta get Ty out of here right now!"

There was no time to waste. Torg snatched his stuff up and dove through the air, landing hard on the ground behind Ty with a thud. No sooner had he hit the ground than a big raptoid spider burst out of the tall grass. Its cold black eyes shined in the fading moonlight as it attacked!

Torg swung his bow and smacked it as hard as he could. It flew through the air with a high-pitched squeal and splattered against the wall of the cavern.

"Ty, wake up!" shouted Torg. "Wake up, wake up!"

But Ty just laid there like a lifeless corpse. So he reached down and grabbed Ty's shield, then leaped over him and readied himself for the fight of his life.

You could hear the grass rippling as the swarm of raptoids scurried toward them. Torg let out a thunderous battle cry as they started to shoot out of the tall grass. Still covered with the morning dew off the grass, Torg smirked in glee because he could still faintly make out their silhouettes as they approached. "Sweet!" mumbled Torg. "I can see you! C'mon, you little freaks! Come and get some."

He swung Ty's shield and slammed the first one so hard that it splattered like an egg, then spun around and slashed the next one in half, sending one side of its body bouncing off the boulder Ty was lying on and the other hitting the ground, twitching as its blue blood oozed out. "Three down, one thousand to go!"

Just then, a wave of raptoids burst out of the grass. Torg had no time to think, no time to call out for help as he raised Ty's shield and drew his sword and started slashing anything that moved. The air filled flooded with the sounds of battle. The screeching of spiders, the crack of the shield, and the sound of his sword slicing and hacking through wave after wave of those monsters. "Hurry up, Normack! I can't hold them back much longer!"

"I'm coming. I'm coming!" Normack cried out as he shot over the boulders next to Torg. "Grab him and jump on!"

Normack quickly coiled up, making a wall between them and the wave of flesh-eating raptoids as Torg struggled to pick Ty up. Then using his tail, Normack frantically started swatting them back and giving him enough time to grab Ty.

"Normack, Ty's not waking up! He's not moving at all."

"Just grab him and throw him over!"

"I've got him. Let's get out of here!" Torg shouted as he flung Ty's body over his shoulder.

"Now hold on tight. If you fall off, you'll be dead before you hit the ground!"

Normack rose up high to protect his precious cargo and took off through the deep grass."

"Just hang on. I'll get us out of here!"

"I'm trying, but Ty's slipping!"

Normack looked back in terror as he slid through the tall grass. The sounds of raptoids popping and squishing beneath Normack sent chills through Torg as he clung on as hard as he could.

"We're almost there!" shouted Normack. "Just a little farther!"

With a last-chance burst, Normack shot into the forest as the sunlight broke through the trees and burnt the last of the raptoids to a smoldering crisp!

"We'll be okay now!" shouted Normack in exhausted relief. "Just stay on my back and hold on to Ty. I'll find us a safe place to rest."

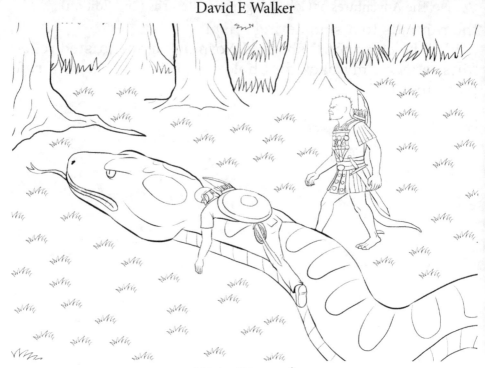

CHAPTER 18
THE MYSTERIES DEEPEN

Normack silently slipped into the fading darkness until he came upon a small clearing next to a slow-moving stream.

"Are you two all right?" whispered Normack as he slowly turned and eased them safely to the ground.

"I'm okay, but Ty still feels really cold. He's not like us. He should be warm all the time!"

"I know that. We have to get him some help. Wait! Look over there next to the stream. If I'm not mistaken, they look like minlar tracks.

"Normack, I don't recognize these tracks. What's a minlar?"

"Minlars are very small creatures, kind of like half-hawk and half-elf. They're an honorable race and very wise. If these are minlar tracks, they might help. That is, if we can find them and if they believe that we are worthy of their help! Stay right here with Ty. It's worth a shot to see where these tracks go. I'll be back soon!"

"All right. Be careful. I'm gonna gather some dry grass and cover him up to keep him warm."

"Good idea. Tuck him in real good!"

"I'd sing him a lullaby too if it would help!"

"No, don't. With a voice like yours, I'm sure it would kill him. Just look after him and I'll be back soon!"

"Whatever!"

All Torg could do now was sit around and wait for Normack to return. Of course, one thing about the Shadow Forest that'll never change is you're never really alone, and no creature will ever turn up an easy meal. So Torg stood guard again, just as he would at the entrance to Zintar.

An hour went by and the warm sun was rising up higher from the east when Ty started to roll over and knocked off the warm grass blanket Torg made for him.

"Hey, dude. Are you all right?" Torg asked as he ran up to his side. "Just stay there and rest some more. Normack went out to get you some help. We were worried about you! How do you feel? Is there anything I can do?"

"I'm okay, Torg. You sound like my Mom," whispered Ty as he rubbed his head and slowly sat up. "I feel like I just got sucker-punched in the head by Pete and Joe. Hey, how did I get here? What's wrong with me? I feel weird."

"That water witch did something to you, and you were out cold all night long. We had to get you out of there fast, so we carried you out!"

Ty just sat there silently for a few more minutes, then grabbed his spear and used it to brace himself as he stood up. His legs were a bit wobbly, and he was still a bit weak. As he looked around, Ty still felt a bit stiff, so he arched his back to stretch out and slowly turned his head to crack his neck.

"I'm still cold, and I'm really hungry. When Normack gets back, let's look around for something to eat!"

"Sounds real good to me!" Torg chuckled as he sat down next to Ty. "I'm so hungry. I'll eat anything!"

"Yeah, me too."

They didn't have long to wait until Normack came slithering back.

"Hey! You're awake! How do you feel, Ty? We were afraid you weren't going to make it!"

"I'm okay. I just want to get out of this place and find

something to eat. What happened to you? It looks like you've gained a few pounds. Or did you eat already?"

"Very funny, fish feet. It just so happens that I did find a little morsel to fill my stomach while I was out. But don't worry, I still saved a little room for you!" Normack said jokingly as he looked down at Ty. "But if it's food you need, there is a field of ripe fruit and apples that can get stuck in your teeth just over that ridge. You remember, just like that apple that got stuck on my fangs!"

Ty smiled and started to laugh. "Yeah, I remember!"

Torg bent down and picked up Ty's shield, then smiled, "Well, if you feel up to some walking, let's head over to that field. Some fresh food sounds really good about now."

Ty nodded and smiled a little as he leaned on his spear.

"Oh yeah," Torg remarked as he walked past Ty. "Whatever happened to those tracks you were following?"

"I don't know. They just disappeared past an old tree. I guess whatever it was must have climbed up or flew away. Let's just grab our stuff and get to that field!"

Normack waited for both of them to gather their things, and when they were ready, he led the way through the forest to a clearing across the stream. "We can cross here. The water is shallow and safe."

"How much farther?" moaned Torg as he gave Ty a nudge.

"Not much," he responded as they splashed their way across the stream. "We have to get to the far side of that cliff up ahead. There's a crack in the wall big enough for us to fit through coming up. When we squeeze through there, then you'll see! The entrance is well hidden, and I don't think we'll have anything to worry about once we get inside."

"Are you kidding me?" snapped Ty. "I don't want to go inside another cave right now!"

"Don't worry. You're going to like it there. I guarantee it!"

After squeezing past thick bushes and crawling over two large trees that must have fallen during a really big storm, Normack turned and went up to the side of the cliff. "There is an entrance around here somewhere."

They looked all around, pulled back some vines, and finally spotted some thick bushes growing right in front of that entrance. It had sharp thorns and twisted vines growing on the walls of the opening.

"How in the world did you find this place, Normack?" asked Torg.

"I could taste the cool fresh air coming out from behind the bushes, and the aroma of fresh fruit made my tongue tingle! You call yourself a Zintarian Guardian. How embarrassing. Can't you taste it with that puny little-forked tongue of yours?"

As they squeezed their way through the crack, they got their first look at the valley and stopped dead in their tracks. It was incredible! Deep green grass flowed gracefully across the ground like a thick blanket, and the trees were filled with all kinds of delicious fruits and berries as far as their eyes could see. There were apples, peaches, honeydrops, cherries, Strawberries, and even wild grapevines crawling wildly up the cliffs' steep walls surrounding the valley. It was like the most beautiful garden you have ever seen.

"Nice job, Normack! This place is awesome!" Ty said, grinning from ear to ear.

Normack had a big grin on his face, too, as he watched them looking around. "You two go and enjoy yourselves. I'm gonna coil up in the grass and warm myself while you two get something to eat!"

"Normack, this place is amazing! Hey, you've been up all night long. Why don't you try to get some rest too?" Torg replied. "It looks like you could use some downtime."

They both watched as he coiled up in the soft grass. Then as soon as he laid his head down, they both shot into the valley like two starving school kids at recess. Sprinting from tree to tree, feasting on the delicious fruits and berries, they headed deeper into the valley without ever looking back.

"Hey, Torg, you got to try these cherries! They're so sweet they taste better than the ones you get on top of an ice-cream Sunday at Uncle John's ice-cream shop. But don't tell him I said that. Okay?"

"I've never tasted so many different things! We don't have this type of food in Zintar. The closest thing we have to cherries are the sweet green grubs that live in the moss in the ceiling above crooked creek. They don't have seeds, but they're pretty fast and you do have to catch them. The worst part is if you're not careful, you'll get stung in your mouth, and your tongue will go numb for hours!"

"You eat grubs? That's gross. I'll never eat a grub no matter how hungry I am!"

"You don't know what you're missing. They might be hard to catch, but they're really good to eat."

"Stop it. Thinking about eating grubs is going to make me puke. Just have another cherry and forget about it."

Ty reached out and grabbed a handful of cherries and threw them at Torg's back. Splat! They hit him right in the back of his head, and that sticky juice started dripping down his neck.

"That's not funny, fish feet! Next time you throw cherries at me, make sure you hit me in my mouth!"

They both started laughing as they sat back in that tree, swinging their legs and plucking cherries.

"Ty, I'm so full I can't eat another bite."

"Me too. This is awesome!"

Ty was feeling much better now. His headache was gone and his belly was full. They stretched out in that tree, finally carefree and relaxed.

It didn't take long until they were fast asleep, but Ty wasn't asleep for very long before he woke up to the sound of a faint voice softly whispering.

"Who's there? Who said that? Hey, wake up. I think I heard something!"

"What is it?" Torg mumbled in a sleepy daze. "I didn't hear a thing!"

"I swear I just heard someone. But it was weird. It kind of sounded like someone said that they wanted to go swimming in . . . lava mud? Pretty weird and creepy, huh? I must have been having a nightmare!"

"Nightmare, are you kidding me? That sounds like a great dream. I was just thinking about taking a nice dip in a steaming pool of lava mud. It would be perfect right now."

"In lava? Are you nuts?"

"Not in real lava. I'm talking about lava mud! You know, that's the mud that bubbles up from the cracks around a stream of molten lava. It's so hot and smooth it takes all of your aches and pains away. You just have to be careful because sometimes lava will gush up into those pools, and, well, have you ever cooked an egg?"

"Dude, you're nuts! I'd never swim in mud. First, being boiled doesn't sound like much fun, and second, my Mom gets mad when my clothes get dirty! I think she would skin me alive if I went and took a bath in mud!"

"Don't knock it until you tried it! Now, why don't you just relax and go back to sleep? You had a rough night and you could use the rest!"

"Hey, I'm not tired anymore. I'm gonna walk around awhile and check out this valley. I'll meet you over by Normack later."

"All right, but don't go too far. After what we've been through, I don't trust any place on the surface land anymore. I swear it's safer walking around the caves near Norgon city than it is up here," he grumbled.

Ty just smiled, then jumped down and headed off to explore the valley. As he got further away from where his friends were, he started thinking about Queen Lylah and everything Torg had done. He wanted to make sure he got back safely to his home and remembered how pleased his Queen was with just a handful of apples he gave her.

Then with a determined grin, Ty ran up to a willow tree that was growing next to a small pond and started snapping small twigs off its flowing branches. "This is going to be perfect," he thought to himself. Then as soon as he had a big pile of fresh twigs, he sat down in the cool shade, stripped the leaves off, and started weaving them into baskets.

Now Ty never made a basket before in his life, but his Mom had some baskets around the house, and he figured it couldn't be any harder than making a net for fishing. So for hours he sat there, twisting and pulling those twigs as best as he could and made two strong baskets with crooked handles on top. He was so proud of himself because they looked strong enough to hold a lot of fresh fruit for their long trip back.

Bubbling With excitement, Ty jumped up, grabbed the baskets, and ran around the valley picking armful after armful of the best fruit he could find. He made sure that they weren't too ripe so they wouldn't spoil while they walked back. He picked apples and honeydrops, cherries, and sugar fruit. In fact, he picked so much fruit that the baskets started to bulge out in the middle. But he wasn't finished yet. Nope! He got down on the ground and started crawling all around, picking up handfuls of seeds from every tree he could find. He filled his pockets until he couldn't put one more seed inside!

Ty could hardly contain his excitement. He snatched up his baskets and flew back to where he left Torg in that cherry tree, but when he got there, he saw that he was already gone. So he just kept his stride and headed back to where they agreed to meet, right outside of the entrance, over by the clearing where Normack was resting. By the time he arrived, his legs were burning and his arms felt like bricks from carrying those heavy baskets across the valley. Normack and Torg didn't even see him coming because they were still sitting with their backs toward him, and it looked like they were just sitting there talking.

"Hey, guys, check out what I've got! I've got an awesome gift for Queen Lylah when we get back!"

"What are you talking about?" muttered Torg as he slowly turned his head.

"This! Check it out. I've picked enough fruit so your whole village can have a feast!"

Ty stopped right next to his friends and dropped his baskets by their feet.

Torg's mouth dropped open, and he couldn't say a word. He just sat there in shock and mumbling.

"What's wrong with him, Normack? I thought he would appreciate this."

"Looks like you finally found a way to shut him up. I think he is in shock."

Torg stood up and gazed in disbelief. "You wish to give this as a gift for my Queen? I can't believe it! This is the most incredible thing anyone has ever offered to a Zintarian Queen! Why would you do that?"

"Are you kidding me? If it weren't for you two, I would be dead, and my home would have been destroyed. This is the least I could do. I'm just embarrassed that I can't do anything more!"

"Again, you honor my Queen and my people. I'm the one that is privileged to be by your side," Torg said in a stern and commanding tone as he knelt on one knee in front of Ty.

"I am too!" whispered Normack as he lowered his head with respect.

"Would you two guys stop it and get up? I think you must have eaten some rotten fruit and got drunk or something. We're a team, and I just wanted to pay her back for letting you help me!"

Just then, Normack saw something out of the corner of his eyes approaching fast from behind Torg. But before he could even flinch, an old minlar flew up, spread its wings out wide, and landed on the stone just across from Torg. Its sharp claws latched onto that stone, like steel clamps, sending small puffs of stone dust drifting up between its talons.

"I have been watching the three of you ever since you left Morella's cavern. My name is Shaw-Shee. Now why are you here?"

"My name is Tyler. This is Torg, Royal Guardian of Zintar, and this is Normack, the bravest vipercon that ever lived. Why have you been watching us?"

"No man-child has ever entered these woods. Your heart is pure, but you are still naive. I needed to see if you were worthy of the tasks ahead of you!"

"Normack, what is he talking about?"

"What do you mean, what is he talking about? What are you talking about? That minlar is just sitting there staring at us?"

"They cannot hear us," Shaw-Shee whispered in his mind. "You have been given the gift of understanding by the water witch, Morella. I needed to know if you deserved such a gift. Now I ask again. Why are you here?"

"What's going on with Ty, Normack?" Torg whispered.

"I don't know. Ty, are you all right?"

"Shhhh, would you two be quiet? It's hard to hear him. I'll tell you in a minute."

Ty told him all about his adventure and why he returned, then asked him if he knew the way back to the Crystal

Mountain.

"The path you seek is not far. Just past the valley is the edge of the great blue fields. You will find a faster and safer route if you travel through the caverns by the northern cliff's edge. But beware. Do not go in too deep. That is also the way back to Norgon city. Stay to the right at the great falls, and you will find your way back. Good luck to you and your friends. We'll be watching!"

With that, Shaw-Shee spread his wings and flew straight up and out of sight.

"What in the world just happened?" snapped Normack. "It looked like you were in a trance!"

"I'm not sure. That minlar was talking to me. I mean, I could hear what it was thinking, and I could talk to him just like I'm talking to you right now, but we weren't really talking. It was like I knew what he wanted, and we understood each other."

"What in the world are you babbling about?"

"I don't know. It doesn't make any sense! He said that I have the gift to understand the thoughts of all creatures, and the water witch, Morella, gave it to me. How does he know about the water witch?"

"Morella. That was Morella?" Torg bellowed out loudly. "Listen to me. Legends say that Morella was cast out from the underworld for her trickery and for empowering others with her magic. If she shared her powers with you back in the cold waters, you have to be careful. Nothing good ever came from her mischief!"

"You must've been hit on the head harder than we thought," teased Normack. "That minlar was just sitting there. If you have the power to read thoughts, then what am I thinking?"

Ty stopped and looked over at Normack, but nothing came to mind. "I don't know, and I don't know what happened to me back there. But I swear he was talking to me. I'm not crazy!"

"Well then, great wizard. What did it say?" Normack snipped with a sarcastic chuckle.

"He told me that he was watching us for a long time, and we would find our way back to the blue fields if we go through the caverns by the northern cliff's edge. I don't know what to believe, guys, but what do we have to lose?"

Normack swayed up and looked over to Torg. "I say we go to the northern cliff's edge. We have nothing to lose, and I'm curious."

CHAPTER 19
THE LAND OF PLENTY

Torg slapped Ty on the back, then grabbed both baskets. "I'll carry these gifts for you. I'm sure your parents would be proud!"

Ty started to blush and smiled a little; he did miss his family a lot. He thought about what his Mom and dad would think about what he was doing and started to laugh as a guilty smirk started to show through. "You have no idea, Torg. If my Mom really knew where I was and what I was doing, she would have a fit! She gets nervous whenever I go fishing by myself. But if she knew we picked a fight against the Norgons and I went after a rinog by myself, I think she would explode! Then I would be grounded until I was ninety."

Normack busted out laughing. "The great Cobasfang, Lord of the Shadow Forest, grounded for life! Locked in his bedroom until he's ninety! I could see you now, hanging out of your window, yelling at everybody that walked by. "Hey, buddy, do you wanna play checkers? I've got some warm milk and cookies!"

"Stop it, Normack. Don't listen to him. We know you wouldn't have warm milk. That would give him gas. There's nothing worse than a ninety-year-old Cobasfang farting in his bedroom!"

"Nice, really nice, guys. I was going to let you two sleepover for a couple years too! My Mom makes great cookies. It wouldn't be so bad."

By the time they stopped teasing him, they were almost at the other side of the valley. The cool shade from the great cliffs gave them a refreshing break from the hot summer sun as they walked through the grass.

"This place is great. I love it here," said Ty with a soft smile. "I'd like to bring my brother here and try some fishing in that pond we passed with all those lily pads floating around. I bet you there's are a lot of huge fish swimming around just waiting to be caught! Hey, Torg, those baskets are pretty heavy. Pass one over. I can carry one for a while."

"No, it's okay. I got it, but do you mind if I use your spear so I could slide it through the handles and sling them across my shoulders?"

"No problem, that's a great idea. Here, catch!"

Torg spun around and snatched the spear as it zipped by his side.

"Dude, that was a little close!"

"Sorry!"

"This is going to work great," said Torg as he slipped it through the handles. "We used to carry our packs like this when we were in training. My Guardian Master would make us run up and down the river's edge like this until one of us fell. Then he would make the rest of us pick him up and carry him too."

Normack looked over and shook his head. "That sounds like too much work!"

"Trust me. It was a lot of work. But it did make us strong." Then he reached down and snatched the baskets off the ground like it was nothing at all. Resting the spear across his strong, broad shoulders and his arms outstretched to help keep his balance, Torg started marching again.

Everyone kept quiet for a while, just walking and enjoying the peacefulness of that valley. They had no worries since they didn't have to keep a lookout for danger, and Torg was smiling all the way. He was so proud of the gifts he was carrying. He started strutting and skipping like a kid. After a little while of walking along the northern's cliff's edge, he leaned over and nudged Ty with one of the baskets.

"You were right, young Cobasfang. I can see an entrance to a cavern up ahead, just where you said it would be, and it looks just wide enough for all of us to fit through."

Normack looked over and saw it too. "I guess the next time he says a little birdie told me, we gotta listen, right Torg?"

"Yeah, I guess so," he chuckled as he nudged Ty again.

As soon as they got there, Torg set the baskets down in the shade and peeked inside the cavern.

"This place smells like rat breath. I guess that's perfect for you Normack, so why don't you go in first? And if you sense any danger at all, just turn around and come right back! We'll stay here and wait for you to check it out."

"No problem. That sounds like a good idea. I'll be back soon. You two get some rest." Then he ducked his head and slowly slithered into the darkness.

Ty took off his sword and bow and tossed them down next to the baskets, then he slid down against the wall and started to bounce a couple of rocks off a stump nearby.

"What's wrong, Ty? You look a little down."

"I always thought the Shadow Forest would be more dangerous to walk around outside and in the open. But let's face it, we got into more trouble walking around in those nasty caves under the Crystal Mountain."

"Ty, you don't have to go. We'll be alright."

"That's not what I mean. I really do want to go back to Zintar with you. I guess I'm just tired of sneaking around and being attacked by rats!"

"I know what you mean. It never was like that before. The Norgon used to be peaceful, and they always left us alone. But that was before Drockmar became in charge. Now all they want to do is raid our villages and steal whatever they can!"

Ty just looked over and threw another rock. "He sounds a lot like a couple of bullies back at home. I hope one day someone will teach them a lesson they'll never forget."

As they rested, Ty started to hear Torg's thoughts. He knew he was missing his people too and longed to feel the peacefulness of his home as well.

"Hey, Torg, do you mind if I ask you a question?"

"No, not at all."

"Where did you get that scar on your back?"

"I got that when a Norgon war party almost killed me. You see, every ten years, when the twin moons and the second planet line up, seven Guardians are chosen to escort five elders to the forbidden shores of the Great Waters. That's where the elders can speak to the creator and ask for his blessings for peace and good fortune, and then the chosen high priest of the elders will receive the creator's guidance and wisdom."

"Wow, that sounds pretty cool!"

"It's one of the most dangerous journeys a Zintarian guard could go on. You see, three years ago, I was chosen to lead the Zintarian Guardians in protecting the elders on their quest. It is an honor to be chosen for this mission."

"You went to the end of the world! What was it like?"

"Like I said, it was real rough. We had to travel right through the heart of the Norgons' country and then past the land of the dead. Over there, the hot winds are filled with sulfur from the lava flows, but that wasn't too bad. The worst part was the cave rats. They were all over the place!"

"How did you get past them?"

"Well, we were armed to the teeth and used up a lot of arrows. They started to leave us alone and feed on the remains of their dead until, one day, they attacked and ripped our supply cart apart before we were able to stop them. They stole half of our food and destroyed all of our water buckets!"

"Why didn't you turn back?"

"We had a mission, and there was no turning back!"

"We traveled using half rations for three days until we made it to the forbidden shore and set up camp. I sent out two of my Guardians to hunt and resupply our food. They were great hunters and did a fine job!"

"Torg, what did they get?"

He started to laugh a bit, then picked up a rock and

skipped it across the ground at that stump too. "I don't have a clue what that thing was that they brought back. All I know is that it had six legs, some really long teeth, but it tasted real good!"

"How did you know it wasn't poisonous?"

"Simple. We gave it to the elders first!" chuckled Torg before he threw another stone. "No, I'm kidding. We cooked it real good and played throw down, and the loser was our taste tester!"

"What's that?"

"It's a game we used to play. You get a board and draw a circle on it, then take one of the jewels out of your sword and spin it real fast. The last person that stays in the circle wins! We used to play it all the time when we were younger."

"That's sound fair, I guess," laughed Ty.

"Seven days passed as we stood guard on the sandy shores until the elders informed us that it was time to return. They did not speak to us anymore on the way back. I feared their prayers were not answered, and peace was not to be in our future."

"They wouldn't even talk to you?"

"No, they just walked back in silence. Every once in a while, one of the elders would chant a little, but that was about it."

"Then what happened?"

"As we entered the land of Norgon, a scout spotted us and sent word of our presence back to Lord Drockmar. He set up an ambush for us as we entered a narrow pass. He must have wanted us to suffer and train his army because he didn't send in his pack of cave rats to cut us apart. He sent in two legions of soldiers instead!

"One came in from in front of us, and one crept up from behind, except I was ready for his attack. I realized that it was too quiet on our return, so I had three of my Guardians dress up like elders, then left the elders and two more Guardians to follow far behind us just in case we were attacked. Scales and I lead the way when the attack happened. We had no chance. Their army came at us from both sides, swinging axes and clubs. I jumped up and sliced my way into their charging hoards. But there were too many!"

171 The Land Of Plenty

"What happened then? And how did you and Scales get away?"

"Well, that was when I felt something sharp slam in my back as a Norgon tried to split me in half with an ax. I must've passed out, and they thought I was dead. When I woke up, I was staring into the faces of our elders helping me, and my Guardians were untying Scales. He was tortured and left in a net nailed to the ground to be eaten alive by insects. We were the only ones that made it. My other Guardians were killed and hacked apart by those monsters!"

"Torg, if you didn't split up like that, your elders would never have made through alive. I'm sorry to hear about your Guardians, but it sounds like they were real heroes, risking their lives to protect others."

Just then, Torg snapped his head back toward the cavern's opening. "Well, Normack's back. I can hear him coming now!"

"It's about time. He was gone a long time!"

Ty stood up and watched as his two great big green eyes slithered out from the shadows of the cave.

"Hey, Normack, remember the last time you sneaked out of a cave at me like that? What took you so long?"

"That's right, little morsel, just stand right there!"

Ty started to laugh and gathered up his things. Then Torg walked over to the baskets and got ready too.

"Two little morsels, that sounds twice as nice!"

As Ty turned around, he saw him slithering out of the cave with his mouth slowly opening.

"Watch out, Torg!" screamed Ty. "That's not Normack!"

Torg wasn't ready for a fight. He was just trying to sling the baskets of fruit over his shoulders when that vipercon snatched him off the ground and wrapped him tight in his grip.

Glancing down as his spear hit the ground, Torg slid his sword from his side and slammed its point deep into the roof of its mouth, just as it struck!

"Bad choice for a meal, rat breath!" shouted Torg. "How does Shear-Akon taste?"

Torg held on tightly and jammed his sword in deeper and deeper as the vipercon's blood gushed out of its mouth.

"Hang on, Torg. I'm coming!"

Before Ty could even grab his sword, the vipercon started to shake and tremble as it lost its grip on life. The battle was already over. Torg had slain a vipercon!

"Torg, are you all right? You were incredible!"

"Help me get out of here, Ty. This thing is crushing me!"

Ty pulled and tugged with all his might as Torg wiggled his way out of its cold dead grasp.

"No wonder why there aren't any rats around here. That cave must've been its home! But if that's its home, then where's Normack?"

"I don't know," Ty shouted back quickly. "Let's go and find out."

There was no time to waste. They snatched everything off the ground and took off into the cave.

Ty pulled out his star crystal and searched every dark slit in the walls of the cave, looking for any sign of Normack.

"He's not here. I don't see him anywhere." Whispered Ty as he snuck further inside. "I think that thing let him go by just so it could sneak up and get us!"

"I think you're right. Normack must be somewhere up ahead at the other end of the cave."

Unfortunately, Ty was right. As soon as they came to the end of the cave and into the huge cavern where the waterfall was, they found Normack lying on the shore of the river, with a spear stuck in his side.

"What in the world happened, Normack? Are you all right?" Ty shouted as he pulled out the spear.

"I'm okay. That toothpick can't pierce my scales. When I came into the clearing, I was jumped on by a sneaky fat little scout. He was hiding behind those rocks by the water's edge and slammed that spear into me before I knew he was there!"

Torg looked all around and then looked back at Normack. "We got to get out of here right now before he reports back to Drockmar!"

"We don't have to worry about that," Normack hissed with a sneaky little smirk. "He's not going to snitch on anyone anymore. I just hope he doesn't give me a stomachache."

They both spun around and looked at Normack. There

definitely was a lump on his side about the size of a Norgon.

"I guess that's one way to keep him quiet," laughed Torg as he shook his head at Normack. "But I prefer the old-fashion way with a spear."

Ty walked over by the falls raining down into the pool of clear water, splashed some water on his face, then cupped his hands and took a refreshing drink. "We got to go to the right and follow the river," he said as he pointed downstream. "Shaw-Shee told me that if we go any farther, we will end up back at Norgon city. I never want to see another Norgon as long as I live, so let's get moving."

"I'm with you. C'mon, Normack, since I'm carrying these baskets, how's about you take the lead again, and Ty can cover our backs?"

Normack simply nodded his head and disappeared into the shadows along the river's edge. The sounds of the waterfall and the river's rippling waters hid the swishing sounds of Normack slithering across the soft sandy beach.

"Torg, we got to be careful. Shaw-Shee told me this would be a shortcut, but Norgons did travel this way a lot. I'm going to use my bow and smooth out the sand behind us to cover our tracks."

"That's a great idea. You're starting to think like a true Zintarian Guardian. But don't make it too clean. A path that has no tracks is a path that will lead your enemy right to you. Do not forget that!"

"I won't. Did your Guardian master teach you that?"

"Nope, Scales did."

The farther they went, the tighter and tighter the walls of that cavern started to close in. They were full of moss and wild poison berries that only grow in damp and musty caves.

"Hey, Torg, check this out! There's some drawing scratched in the wall behind that moss."

"You're right. It looks like some of the old scratchings we used to find near the lava pits when I was a kid."

"C'mon, let's keep going. The river's slowing down, and I think I can smell some fresh air!"

"I hope you're right. It would be nice to get out of here without running into any more Norgons."

"Just don't slow down and we will be out of here soon. I can definitely smell some fresh air trickling in."

Moments later, Torg stopped and started to smile. "Hey, Ty, I can see some light coming up ahead. We must be getting close."

"Not soon enough for me. I can't wait till I feel the warm sun again!"

"Torg, I'm not sure which way to go. The cave breaks off in two directions. Do you want to split up? You can take the right trail, and I'll take the left?"

"I have a better idea. Grab one of those stones and throw it as hard as you can against the ceiling. Let me show you a trick."

Ty shrugged his shoulders and figured he had nothing to lose. So he did just what Torg asked. He picked up a good-sized rock and threw it as hard as he could. Crack! It hit the ceiling and split into three pieces.

Like an explosion of horror, thousands of vampire bats came streaming out of their hiding places right above their heads. Screeching and flapping, they took off like a massive cloud out the right cave.

"Well, Ty, that's the way out. Just follow the screeching because I guarantee you, they're headed out of here as fast as they can fly!"

"Nice trick. I've gotta remember that one! Hey look, there's Normack. Hey, Normack, we made it!"

"You were right, Ty," remarked Normack. "That cave led us to the edge of Grog's land, and I can see the blue fields from here. The thing is, it looks like we won't be able to get across from here. We'll have to head down into the ravine and go the long way around."

"Not today Normack. I'm not walking around Grog's land anymore. You two can just stay here. If I'm not back in a few minutes, then you guys can go the long way, and I'll see you on the other side of life. Because I'm not gonna let Grog push us around anymore!"

Ty boldly walked out of the cave and into the field of rocks and boulders straight into Grog's territory. "Hey, Grog!" shouted Ty. "Are you here? Come on out. Wake up, boulder butt."

The ground started to rumble under Ty's feet once more as Grog lumbered up, turned around, then stomped a jagged boulder into dust.

"Now look Grog, if it wasn't for us, you'd still be trapped in the Norgons' arena. We ain't gonna hurt you. We just wanna walk to the blue fields so we can get to the Crystal Mountain. If you wanna fight, then we'll fight, but I would rather ask for your permission. So, what is it going to be? Will you please let us pass?"

Grog stood there silently for a moment, then sat back down and rested. Ty could hear his thoughts more clearly than he ever heard anyone else's before. He knew that Grog appreciated being freed, and he gave them his permission to cross.

"Thank you, Grog. If you ever need my help, I'll come and stand by your side like you stood by ours!"

Grog nodded his head as if he understood every word, and he laid back down. There was no more anger in Grog's heart. He was calm and at peace.

"C'mon, guys, everything's okay. Grog's gonna let us cross his land. He wanted to thank us for freeing him, and he's just laid back down to get some sleep, so let's go!"

"Normack, that young man-child has more guts than any creature I know. I don't think anybody will ever believe me when I tell them what we just saw!"

"I know what you mean. I saw it, and I still don't believe it!" snickered Normack softly after flicking his tongue a few times. "Now let's get going before Grog gets back up and changes his mind!"

"I'm with you, buddy," grunted Torg, just before he cupped his hands over his mouth and shouted back to Ty. "Hey, Ty, we'll be right there. I just have to grab your baskets."

"What do you mean my baskets? They're our baskets." Ty shouted back. "Now c'mon and hurry up!"

Torg and Normack just looked at each other, then shook their heads and grinned. When they finally got to Ty, he was just sitting down, waiting and swinging his feet back and forth.

"Let's get out of here, Ty," Normack hissed in a soft, sharp voice. "I don't want Grog to get upset, so let's get going."

"Don't worry, he's fine. In fact, I'm sitting on his belly right now."

"You're sitting on what?" Torg shouted as he stumbled backward. "Did you just say you were sitting on Grog's stomach? Just sitting there swinging your legs like you were on some swing somewhere?"

"Yep, I told you that I talked to him, and he said he was glad that we helped him out. Don't worry about Grog. He's pretty cool. All he wants to do is chill out. He just gets upset when something messes with his sleep. So let's leave him alone and get back to Zintar."

Torg looked over at Normack and shrugged his shoulders.

"Let's get moving then. We can be back in an hour with a little luck."

"Now that's what I'm talking about!" Grinned Ty as he slid down Grog's belly. "I'll see ya later boulder butt, and I hope you get some sleep." Then he turned and slapped Grog right on his belly as he walked away, heading straight for the blue fields with his friends.

CHAPTER 20
TO KILL A VIPERCON

The walk back through Grog's land to the blue fields went by faster than before. They all were bubbling with excitement as they realized their adventure was almost over.

Ty took the lead and marched with his shoulders straight and his head held high as they made it to the grassy edge of the blue fields.

"We're finally back where we started, Normack!"

"You're right, and I think we must've walked completely around the Shadow Forest by now!"

"Hey, Torg," Ty exclaimed, "let me show you something."

"What is it?"

"Over there, next to that pillar is where I killed that life leech. Let's check it out! I wonder if there's anything left of it after it's been lying out here so long!"

"All right, let's go."

Torg was eager to check out the place that he had heard

so much about, so when Ty started to pick up his pace, he was right behind him step by step. Normack, on the other hand, wasn't too anxious to see that life leech again. He wouldn't mind it a bit if he never saw another one of those things again for the rest of his life.

When they were about halfway there, Torg looked back and nodded to him to hurry up. "C'mon, slowpoke, I don't want to lose you now!"

"What are you talking about? You couldn't lose me if you tried! I could follow the scent of those smelly armpits of yours even if I was underwater and had a dead sludge tarpon strapped to my face!"

"Are you kidding me? A dead sludge tarpon strapped to your face would be an improvement!"

"Hey, sounds like you two should get married!

"Good idea, Ty. Let me wrap a ring around his neck!"

"Very funny, like you could afford one!"

Ty ran right up to the spot where he had killed that thing and looked all over. "Normack, it's gone! There's nothing left. Something must have come over here ate everything up!"

"You're right," Normack replied as he stopped next to Ty. "Whatever did that must've been really hungry!"

"Scavenger beetles," grunted Torg as he pointed at the loose dirt. "Look, there's no big tracks around, and the top layer of dirt is gone. Those things don't mess around when they strip a carcass clean. They take everything!"

Suddenly, Ty looked over at Normack and sat back down on the edge of the crystal. "I just remembered something. I don't think you can come with us to Zintar!"

Torg put the baskets down and put his hands on Ty's shoulders. "What are you talking about? He'll be welcomed to my land!"

"I'm talking about the cave!" Ty snapped back as he threw a small piece of crystal across the ground. "Don't you remember? He'll never fit down the crack that leads to the river. He's too big!"

"Relax, young Cobasfang warrior, I was thinking about that too, and there's another way back!"

"Where? We looked all over this mountain, and that was

the only cave that led into the underground tunnels!"

"Don't you remember when Scales and I climbed up the far side of the cliff? I saw an old lava tube next to the wall behind where you were sitting. We can go down it and find another way back. Even if it goes all the way to the fire river, I'm sure I can get us back!"

Normack stood up and shook his head. "No, I'll stay out here again. I don't want you to take a dangerous path just so I can come along. It's more important to get Torg back safely with your gifts."

"Would you two trust me? I'd rather go back that way anyway. Going back the same way we went before would not be smart. Norgon hunting parties go there a lot, so the lava tube would be a lot safer."

"All right then," Ty said as he stood up and slung his bow over his shoulder. "Let's get going!"

Ty jumped down and took the lead while Torg was adjusting the baskets on the spear. "Don't wait for me. I'm right behind you!"

It was a real short trip back to the hidden entrance Ty had found so long ago. The splintered branches were still scattered across the ground where he chopped his way through. "We made it, guys!" screamed Ty as he darted through the brush. "C'mon, we're almost there!"

Normack smiled and ducked his head as he glided through the opening. "So this is what that cavern looks like. The way you were talking about it, I thought it would've been smaller!"

"This is where we had our first run-in with that rinog," Ty explained as he showed him the slash marks on the crystal walls from their fight.

"With all these snapped arrows around, it looks like you guys had your hands full!"

"You're right about that," boasted Torg as he walked by both of them. "We were lucky to make it out of here alive. Now follow me and I'll show you where that tunnel is."

Ty started to grin and ran up next to Torg as they approached the tunnel. "Hey, how about handing me one of those baskets, please? There's no way you'll fit inside carrying them that way. Besides, I think it'll be easier if we drag the baskets. The tunnel is as smooth as glass, and if we tie my rope around them, we can pull them behind us."

"Listen to him Torg. He's making a lot of sense. It would be a lot easier that way."

"All right then. Toss me an end and I'll tie it off."

Seconds later, Torg had his basket secured and started to head down the tunnel with Ty close behind. However, Normack stayed back a little just in case the tunnel became too narrow, so he could turn around and not get stuck.

The tunnel was perfectly round, and every little sound seemed to ping off its walls like a marble in a glass as they cautiously made their way back into Torg's land. It was the easiest path they had ever taken.

While they traveled, Torg explained that the tunnel was created millions of years ago when lava burned its way through the rock and helped create the Crystal Mountain.

"I've been in a tunnel like this before," Normack hissed softly from behind. "We have to be really careful. The ground might look strong, but it could shatter at any time. I chased a proglidon down one of these tunnels before, and it fell through the floor before I could catch it."

"They could get pretty big. How big was it?" Torg asked.

"It was a good-sized one and would have made a good meal, about the size of a bull sloth, I guess."

"Well, I don't think we have to worry about that, Normack. They weigh a lot more than we do, and they stomp hard when they walk."

Ty looked back and didn't say a word. The scratching sounds of the baskets dragging across the ground made it a little hard to hear what everyone was saying. So everyone just kept on going and enjoyed the smooth path they chose.

"We must be getting closer to the great fire river," Torg finally pointed out. "I can feel the heat and the air is getting dry."

"Is that close to Zintar?" Ty asked.

"Yeah, not far at all. There's a tunnel there that'll lead us to the far side of the gates of Zintar. The only problem will be crossing the river."

"Wait, you didn't say anything about crossing a river of fire, and I'm guessing you're talking about a river of lava," snapped Ty.

"Don't worry about it until we get there. It all depends on how fast it's flowing. On a good day, when it flows soft and slow, there is a bridge we can use to get across, but when the river is angry, and the fire is too close, we'll just have to find another way around."

"Sounds a bit dangerous to me," Ty chuckled as he looked back at Normack. "And you guys say I take too many chances!"

"Looks to me like Ty's rubbing off on you a little bit, Torg. I hope you know what you're doing."

"I know what I'm doing! The fire river is right up ahead. I can see the red glow from here!"

"You're right. I can see it too. Hey, Normack, wait till you see it. There's a huge cavern up ahead that looks like it's covered in black glass. The whole place is glistening red and orange, and there's a huge river of lava flowing right down the middle!"

He hurried up and quickly caught up to them and lay down by their sides, amazed by the sheer beauty of the cavern.

"I've seen many tunnels and caverns in my life, but this one is the most magnificent one of them all! Now, where's that bridge you were talking about?"

Torg turned and pointed downstream. "Down there, the cavern narrows where an ancient column fell across. We can cross there! And Ty, let me have the basket back now. It'll be easier for me to keep my balance while we walk across the black glass if I carry them both."

Ty agreed and untied his basket, then coiled up his rope and slung it over his shoulder again.

"Be very careful!" warned Torg. "The ground is very slippery, and if you fall, you'll land in the river. I have lost two of my fellow Guardians that way!"

The path along the river of fire was steep and slippery. Ty was using his spear to help him keep his balance while Torg struggled as the baskets swung back and forth. They made their way over slick boulders and hopped across large gaps in their path.

"Torg, wait up!" Ty finally spoke up. "I don't want you to

slip and fall. Those baskets aren't worth it."

"I'll be okay! Just don't come too close. If I fall, I don't wanna knock you over!"

"I've got an idea. Let's tie my rope around you, so if you fall, you won't land in the river!"

"Listen to him, Torg. Our young warrior is finally using his head! We've come too far together to lose you now."

"All right, just be careful!"

Ty gently tied himself off, and cinched the other end around Torg nice and tight. "We're in this together now, so if you fall, remember to let go of the baskets, okay?"

Normack smiled as they continued across the river's edge. It was flowing softly, but the heat was almost unbearable even for a cold-blooded serpent like him.

"I can see the bridge from here!" shouted Torg. "We're almost there!"

"I can see it too, but look, it's missing a piece in the middle!"

"It was never like that before. Something must've happened!"

As they made their way to the bridge, they could see a portion missing from the center. Its black glassy arch was wide and strong, but a section was broken off in the center that was too wide to jump over.

"We have to find another way around," Ty said disappointedly as he stabbed his spear into the ground. "We can't risk crossing here!"

"We must try," Normack spoke out as he made his way up to those two. "This ground is too slippery, and I watched as you both almost fell countless times. I can make it past that small break, and you two can cross over me!"

"That's crazy! C'mon, Ty, let's keep going. I'll find us another way across!"

"No, he's right, and you know it! He can do this, and I trust him."

"I trust him too, but we have to be fast. The river can grow angry any minute and wash him off without warning!"

"Well, let's stop talking and get moving!"

Normack slid past them and slowly made his way across the bridge. The river sparkled and flickered with orange fire as it flowed just a few feet beneath him. Then as soon as he reached the gap, he coiled up and shot across without a second's hesitation. He wrapped around the other side as tightly as he could, then shouted out when he was ready. "Ty, you go first. You're the lightest, and when you get across, I want you to tie the rope off just in case I fall!"

"You got it," he replied as he started to crawl across Normack's powerful back. "I'll see you on the other side!"

He crawled as fast as he could, trying not to slip off his shiny hard scales.

"Hurry up, little one. It's starting to get a bit hot down here!"

Ty slid as fast as he could, then as soon as he made it safely across, he untied his rope from around his waist and threw it over a chunk of stone and held on tight.

"It's your turn now. Be careful!"

Torg dropped the baskets and told Ty to hold on for a second as he tied them up tight. "We can pull them across together when I get to the other side!" he commanded in his grumbly stern voice.

"Hurry up, Torg. I'm burning up down here!"

Torg didn't waste another second. He knelt like a runner in a race, then used his sharp talons to scurry across his friend's back in a flash.

"Holy smokes, that was fast!" shouted Ty as he watched him zip across.

"C'mon, Normack, were both across. Let's go!"

Normack slowly started to unwind himself from the side of the bridge just as a crash rang out across the cavern.

"Hurry, Normack!" screamed Torg. "Something smashed into the river, and there's a wave of fire coming right at you!"

As he turned and looked, all he could see was a wall of glowing red lava streaking right for him. "Get out of here!" he shouted as he spun his way across the gap. "And get inside the cave where it's safe!"

Torg spun around and shoved Ty into the cave as Normack came rushing by.

"Get inside, you fool! You're gonna get yourself killed!" Normack shouted as Torg reached to untie the rope.

"I didn't carry it this far to watch it burn up in the river of fire!"

Just as the wall of lava boiled up high in the cavern, he snatched the rope off and shot for safety. "Pull with all your might!" shouted Torg as he tossed the end to Normack. "We can't let it burn!"

With every ounce of energy they had left, they snapped the rope as hard as they could and snatched it across the river as the wave of fire engulfed the bridge.

"You two are nuts!" Ty shouted as he picked himself off the floor. "You said I was crazy and didn't think things through. If either one of you ever says that about me again, I'll hit you with one of those apples!"

"That's a deal," snarled Torg as he crawled back to his feet. "These baskets are more precious than you could ever imagine. I wasn't going to let them burn without a fight!"

"Well Torg, lead the way," Normack hissed softly as he rose up and looked down the tunnel. "We have a gift to give, and I can't wait to see your Queen's reaction."

"Then follow me."

All three walked proudly, side by side, with their heads held high, as they finally entered the land of Zintar. The tunnel was smooth and clean, with fresh air sweeping through. It didn't take long until they could see the dim light of the torches that lined the walls of the great gates flickering in the distance.

"Look, Torg, there's your home. We made it!" Ty said with an eager grin. "Thank you for everything!"

"It was my duty and my pleasure to stand by your side young warrior!"

Normack smiled as he watched them head into the cavern in front of the gates. His heart was full of pride as they slowly approached the century.

"Who goes there?" came a thunderous voice from on top of the wall.

"It is I, Torg Rockmar, Royal Zintarian Commander! I am escorting two royal guests of Queen Lylah! Open the gates!"

"Show us your proof, Commander!" the guard snapped back in disbelief.

As Torg looked over at Ty, he stepped aside and bowed his head.

"I am Cobasfang, lord of the Shadow Forest, open your

gates!" shouted Ty with pride and determination, then held up his fist and showed the guard his ring.

"Open the gates! The Queen has visitors!" commanded the Guardian. "Sound the horns, and prepare the Royal Zintarian guards for an escort!"

The thick iron gates creaked and popped as they swung wide against the tall stone walls. Torg stood tall with Normack by one side and Ty by his other. The sounds of the trumpets that blow for the arrival of royalty echoed across the land as the shadowy figures of the Royal Zintarian Guardians approached.

"This is so cool," Ty muttered as he looked over at Torg with a grin a mile wide. "I feel like a King!"

He just smiled and put the baskets on the ground. "You two are our guests. Now follow me. The Queen awaits your arrival."

As their escorts arrived, Torg looked up and saw his old friend approach. "Scales, good to see you again, my good friend. I cannot wait to tell you all about our journey!"

"Where have you been? We went back to search for you, and you disappeared into the forest. I thought that rinog killed you!"

"We nearly were. It's a long story, but the blue fire rubies were delivered as commanded. This young man-child has the heart of a dragon beating in his chest!"

"And who is this with you over there?"

"This is Normack. He has traveled with us and fought by our side like a true warrior. He is my friend and our guest."

"It is an honor to meet you Normack. Commander Rockmar is a hard one to impress! Guardians, pick up their things and take them to the palace, and Commander, if you would follow me, the Queen is waiting for your arrival."

Ty turned and looked over at Normack as they marched through the courtyard. "Commander? I didn't know we had to salute him!"

"That would explain why he's always barking out orders all the time," Normack snickered as he smacked Ty in his back with his tail.

"Hup, two, three, four," giggled Ty as they walked up the stairs of the great hall.

"Shhhh. You two are embarrassing me. You're acting like children!"

"Sorry, Daddy," snickered Ty as they walked through the golden doors of the Queen's throne room.

As they entered, Queen Lylah was standing at the edge of a long and magnificent table with her royal court by her side.

"I have heard word about your travels from an acquaintance of yours. I am pleased to see that you have returned."

"Your Majesty," Torg spoke softly as he bowed down on one knee. "Cobasfang, Lord of the Shadow Forest, has brought you a great gift in your honor."

"Well then, bring forth the gift and let me see."

"Bring in the basket," ordered the sentry at the door.

As the doors swung open, two guards started marching down the red carpet, then placed the baskets gently in front of the Queen.

Her eyes grew wide and twinkled with joy as she witnessed the magnificent bounty that was laid before her.

"I have never seen so much of these delicacies before. Why have you brought me such an elaborate gift? Were the blue fire rubies not enough for you?"

"The rubies you gave to me were plenty, your Majesty. I wish to offer these two small baskets to you and your people for sending Torg to help me. Without him, I would've never have made it back to my home alive. He risked his life for me many times, and I wished to repay you for that."

"Step closer, Commander. For your honor and bravery, you have earned the respect and gratitude of the people of Zintar. Rise and be known from this day forward as High Commander Rockmar of the Royal Zintarian Guardians!"

Torg looked over at his friends, shocked and surprised. His mouth was hanging open, and you could see his tail shaking nervously.

"Congratulations, Torg," Ty said softly as he bowed his head gently at him. "You have brought honor to your Queen and your people."

"Let there be a feast for all Zintarians. We must celebrate the return of these three heroes!"

"Wait, your Majesty. I have one more gift for your people,"

muttered Ty as he walked up to the edge of the table. "These are the seeds of the trees that produce the fruit we have brought you. If you plant them and keep them watered, they'll grow and supply your people with enough food to live well on." Then as he reached in his pocket, he spilled out mounds of seeds and scattered them across the table."All you need is someplace that has a lot of light and good soil."

"This one is full of surprises, I see," smiled Queen Lylah as she ran her fingers through the seeds.

"You have no idea," chuckled Normack as he gave Torg a sharp poke in his side.

"Take them to the hall of light and do what he says," ordered the queen. "We have a lot to be grateful for today!"

Torg walked over to Ty and put both hands on his shoulders. "Thank you for what you have done for my people. I will never forget it!" while giving Torg a subtle nod.

But as they were walking out of the throne room, a lone sentry came rushing in.

"Queen Lylah," he shouted as he knelt to the floor. "We have captured a Norgon scout just outside of the gates. He says there's a legion approaching from the west, and they're going to destroy your kingdom just like someone that wears your Royal Seal had destroyed theirs!"

Ty stopped, then slowly turned his head as the words of the sentry echoed across the room. The flickering light from the torches froze in silence as Ty gazed back at Queen Lylah.

Taking a soft breath, Ty bowed his head, then slowly wrapped his fingers around the hilt of his sword. "Looks like Lord Drockmar needs to be taught another lesson," he whispered as a sneaky little grin crept from the corner of his mouth. The legend of Cobasfang will continue.

THE FEATURES OF CREATURES

A DETAILED INDEX OF THE INDIGENOUS CREATURES THAT INHABIT THE SHADOW FOREST BY SHAW-SHEE

DYLAN;

Parents unidentified; male of the human species approximately 5'7" tall, deep brown eyes not adapted for seeing underground and with a small patch of fur on its head. Covered with a thin fleshy outer membrane easily penetrated with edged weapons. Has no natural enemies or useful biological appendages to be exploited by any other species. Though an adolescent of the species, it is well adapted with two hands to grasp and construct weapons to hunt or alter the environment. Easily succumbs to injury from poison or venom. Diet; Meat, fruits, vegetables, and as much snacks as he can get his hands on. Notable Attributes; Takes time to make decisions, highly motivated, and extremely dedicated to friends and family, and highly competitive with video games and two-wheeled devices.

GROG;

Male of the Saxun-Inorganicus species approximately 8'11" tall. Large red eyes perfectly adapted for seeing underground. Fortified with a dense outer membrane of stone and invulnerable from strikes from sharp objects. It has no natural enemies, but its biological appendages can be harvested by other species to create bludgeoning weapons. It is well adapted with two hands used to grasp or. Immune to poison or venom. Diet; Salt stone, golden crystals, and occasionally some soft Paka Root. Notable Attributes; Highly territorial and will attack anything that enters its realm.

LORD DROCKMAR;

Male of the Norgon subterranean insect species is referred to as a chimera due to being genetically mutated with the characteristics of the rat-ridder and warrior class of its species. This genetic alteration endowed him with alternating biological appendages due to variations in temperature during gestation. Standing approximately 5'11" tall, highly developed large insect red eyes capable of seeing 140° and perfectly adapted for seeing underground. Fortified with a thick outer membrane of an exoskeleton with poisonous spikes on his backs and capable of resisting penetration from edged weapons which also makes him almost impervious to injury from poison or venom. Due to its classification as a chimera, it was spawned with one thick and strong claw capable of grasping, crushing and using weapons and one saw shaped pincer capable of stabbing and slicing flesh. He has no natural enemies or useful biological appendages to be exploited by any other species. Diet; Small insects, flesh of any consistency, fruits, and fond of spiked slugs. Notable Attributes; He's smart, cunning, and holds an insatiable desire to control all species.

MORELLA;

Parents unidentified and female of the water witch species. Approximately 5'5" tall, deep green eyes adapted for seeing underwater with a small patch of long golden fur on her head. Covered with a thin fleshy outer membrane easily penetrated with edged weapons from the waist to her head. Covered with a thin scales' outer membrane from her waist down to the tip of her tail. Has no natural enemies or useful biological appendages to be exploited by any other species. Though an adolescent of the species, she's well adapted to her environment with two hands to grasp and alter the environment with the use of charms, sorcery, and magic. Easily succumbs to injury from edged weapons, poison, or venom. Diet; Small fish, fruits, and an occasional trespasser. Notable Attributes; Highly territorial and currently banished from the underworld for her unrelenting deceptions towards unsuspecting sentient beings and for empowering others with her sorcery.

NORGON CITY;

A subterranean city populated by approximately 76,000 Norgons. Located deep within The Shadow Forest and buried approximately ½ mile under the Great Crystal Mountain. The city is well fortified with tall stone walls spanning the width of a large cavern, and its entrance is secured with large and rusty iron gates. The only light available and commonly in use are small torches and the occasional burning of trash piles. The insect creatures that dwell within its walls live in dilapidated shakes while its streets and alleys are almost unpassable and infested with insects and rodents of all sizes. Located in the rear of the city and close to the side of the cavern is an arena constructed from stone and iron used for disciplinary actions and/or entertainment that usually ends up with the death and dismemberment of the creatures cast into it. Notable Attributes; The Norgon species used to have a productive and mutually beneficial relationship with the Zintarian race as it pertains to their food sources and maintenance efforts of their city. The Norgons at one time worked alongside the Zintarians in the subterranean orchards and were tasked with keeping the evasive species away from the fruit trees and gardens. Then when it came to harvest time, both species would share the food equally. However, when Lord Drockmar came into power, he claimed the whole area as Norgon property, killed all Zintarians that tried to harvest the crops, then consumed the entire field leaving only dirt and stone behind. This action caused mass starvation in both species and caused the Norgons to adapt a primal scavenging and raiding existence.

NORGONS;

Norgons are identifiable within three sub-species; Rat Riders, Warriors, and Workers. They are a subterranean insect species that travel in packs and resemble a common praying mantis. Averaging between 4'3" to 5'7" tall. Highly developed large insect red eyes capable of seeing 140° and perfectly adapted for seeing underground. Fortified with a thick outer membrane of an exoskeleton with poisonous spikes on their backs and capable of resisting penetration from edged weapons which also makes them almost impervious to injury from poison or venom. They have no natural enemies or useful biological appendages to be exploited by any other species. Dependent upon the sub-species, they are capable of having two or more biological appendages of either hand to grasp and construct weapons or claws/pincers used for crushing or digging. Diet; Small insects, flesh of any consistency, fruits, and fond of bone marrow. Notable Attributes; Difficult to kill even after losing a couple of appendages. They survive by scavenging and plundering and are highly territorial but mildly aggressive when undisturbed and extremely dedicated to hatchling care and development.

NORGON RAT RIDERS;

The first of three subsect species of the Norgon race. A highly developed subterranean insect species averaging between 4'6" to 5'2" tall and well adapted with two hands, and large insect red eyes capable of seeing 140° and perfectly adapted for seeing underground. Fortified with a thick outer membrane of an exoskeleton with poisonous spikes on their backs and capable of resisting penetration from edged weapons which also makes them almost impervious to injury from poison or venom. They have no natural enemies or useful biological appendages to be exploited by any other species. Common weapons used, recurve bow, and double-sided arming sword. Diet; Small insects, flesh of any consistency, fruits, and fond of bone marrow. Notable Attributes; Most intelligent of the species. Highly developed dexterity with their hands which allows them to use tools and manufactured weapons and are capable of directing attack formations and controlling the movements of cave rats as they ride them.

NORGON WARRIOR;

The second of three subsect species of the Norgon race. The tallest and most highly developed subterranean insect species averaging between 5'4" to 5'7" tall and well adapted with two thick and strong claws/pincers and large insect red eyes capable of seeing 140° and perfectly adapted for seeing underground. Fortified with a thick outer membrane of an exoskeleton with poisonous spikes on their backs and capable of resisting penetration from edged weapons which also makes them almost impervious to injury from poison or venom. They have no natural enemies or useful biological appendages to be exploited by any other species. Common weapons used are their thick and strong claws/pincers used to rip, stab and tear flesh. Diet; Small insects, decayed flesh of any consistency, fruits, and fond of bone marrow and flying vertebrae. Notable Attributes; Least intelligent of the species with a highly developed dexterity with their claws and pincers and prone to attack with brute force.

NORGON WORKER;

The third of three subsect species of the Norgon race. Smallest of the three sub-species averaging between 4'3" to 5'1" tall, have hands instead of claws, large insect red eyes capable of seeing 140°, and perfectly adapted for seeing underground. Fortified with a thick outer membrane of an exoskeleton with poisonous spikes on their backs and capable of resisting penetration from edged weapons which also makes them almost impervious to injury from poison or venom. They have no natural enemies or useful biological appendages to be exploited by any other species. Common weapons used are anything available or left behind. Diet; Small insects, flesh of any consistency, and fond of half-decayed meat. Notable Attributes; Average intelligence rating with a highly developed dexterity with their hands. They serve as their building, tunneling, and weapons-making breed.

NORMACK;

Male of the Vipercon species measuring slightly larger than most at approximately 50' long from nose to end of his tail. It has evolved four six-inch-long fangs that can regrow quickly when one lost after a strike, and large green eyes perfectly adapted for low light and seeing underground. Fortified with a thick outer membrane of scales with brownish spots swirling across its muscular back and capable of resisting penetration from edged weapons which also makes them almost impervious to injury from poison or venom. A full-grown dragon is its only known natural enemy. Its scales can be harvested by other species to be used as shields as well as its venom can be harvested as the poison used for arrow tips. Diet; Any warm-blooded creature still alive but prefers large cave rats and bull sloths. Notable Attributes; Known to occasionally invade and hunt domesticated livestock. Considered one of the deadliest of the snake species due to the amount of venom excreted per bite and renowned for being honest and loyal as well as having big appetites and bad tempers.

SHAW-SHEE;

Male of the Minlar species approximately 2' tall with broad feathered wings and resembles a half-hawk and half-elf. Large blue eyes perfectly adapted for low light environments, soft brown and white spotted feathers covering its wings and back. Strong yellow talons that grow to 2" in length. A thin covering of feathers provides a thin layer of protection from penetration due to venomous bites or edged weapons. Tree-born venomous snakes, terrordons, and raptor birds are their only known natural enemy. Diet; Fruits and vegetables with the occasional insect. Notable Attributes; An honorable race, very wise, and overseers for the Shadow Forest laws. The Minlar race also have telepathic abilities strong enough to converse with all sentient beings, as well as having the power to heal minor injuries.

TORG ROCKMAR;

Commander of The Royal Zintarian Guardians and 1st class Assassin. Male of the Zintarian reptiloid species approximately 6'3" tall with a strong tail and a long deep scar across his back. Thinly scaled body able to resist most venomous bites and glazing blows from edged weapons. He is proficient in the use of recurve bow and carries a double-sided arming sword named "Shear-Akon" passed down to him from his father and uses chest plate armor made of rinog hide. Diet; Small insects, small warm-blooded creatures, fruits, and fond of mealworms, crickets, and sweet green grubs. Notable Attributes; Has an unwavering dedication for the protection and defense of the Zintarian Nation and holds keeping his word and the honor of the Zintarians above his own mortality. Also, he is an excellent strategist in battlefield tactics, has a twisted sense of humor, and enjoys teasing his fellow friends.

TYLER;

Commonly referred to as Ty, a male of the human species approximately 5'4" tall, with deep brown eyes not adapted for seeing underground and with a small patch of wavy fur on its head. His father's name is Cobias, and his mother's name is Marie. He has 2 sisters Cristan and Kelly, and a brother named Bobby. Covered with a thin fleshy outer membrane easily penetrated with edged weapons. Though an adolescent of the species, it is well adapted with two hands to grasp and construct weapons to hunt or alter the environment and easily succumbs to injury from poison or venom. While traveling through The Shadow Forest, he possesses and is efficient with a recurve bow as well as a double-sided arming sword created from the hide of a life leach and cured with the power of golden crystals on the cusp of the Crystal Mountain. He also possesses chest plate armor and a shield made from the cured hide of a life leach. Diet; Meat, fruits, vegetables, and as much snacks and ice cream he can get his hands on. Notable attributes; Quick to make decisions but shows high potential for leadership in battlefield statistics. Highly motivated and less likely to take advice but is extremely dedicated to friends and family.

HUMAN VILLAGE;

A land-based city populated by approximately 91,000 human species as well as 26,000 various other sentient species. Located next to a large body of fresh water and borders the western rim of The Shadow Forest. The city is adequately fortified with a thick row of razor bushes spanning the width of The Shadow Forest to the shore of the water. The light most commonly in use are large glowing objects not powered by any known crystals. The inhabitants within its walls reside in housing structures constructed with dead trees that can accommodate one to three "family units" on each level. Located in the center of the community and close to a large transport vehicle that walks on a steel path is a large open field used for recreation and large gatherings. Food distribution locations are dispersed throughout the region and are controlled by the resident of each location. The human species have a wide range of belief structures and often show conflict on their differences. The ruling political and sociological sects are referred to as Governors who are chosen by the inhabitants for a pre-determined length of time. This species is highly devoted to their offspring; however, they do force them to leave their shelters daily at gather in hardened structures of stone and forced to sit in chairs for the duration of the day. Notable attributes; This species is highly developed and routinely changes their environment to suit their needs by sorcery (which they refer to as technology) and manipulate metal and wood to suit their needs. This species was allowed to colonize the lower region of this valley under the conditions laid out in the peace treaty signed by the King of Zintar, their Elders, and the Regent of Norgon. This treaty had the most notable stipulation of; 1) All species could conduct free trade between their colonies as long as they had a mutual agreement. 2) Each species would remain in the region they had laid claim to and not encroach on the territory of others, and 3) The human species could not utilize its technological advantages against any other species unless that species is also in possession of that technology. This last stipulation required the Human species to remove all weapons that fire/project metal to hunt or engage in war and restricts its use of lifeless horses within the realm of The Shadow Forest.

XAVIER;

Parents unidentified, male of the species approximately 5'4" tall, deep brown eyes not adapted for seeing underground and with a small patch of short fur on its head. Covered with a thin fleshy outer membrane easily penetrated with edged weapons. Though an adolescent of the species, it is well adapted with two hands to grasp and construct weapons to hunt or alter the environment and easily succumbs to injury from poison or venom. While traveling through his home village, he possesses and is efficient with a 4" knife and is known to be proficient with a pump-action pellet gun. He is extremely efficient in hunting small game and fishing during the summer months. However, no armament currently in use. Diet; Meat, fruits, some vegetables, and as much snacks he can get his hands on. Notable attributes; He Does not indulge in lengthy conversations that he considers unimportant, is highly motivated to learn new things and is extremely dedicated to friends and family.

NOTEWORTHY CREATURES;

CAVE RAT;

A subsect of the subterranean Magnus Rodentus species that travel in packs and resemble a common rodent. The common male of the species can grow to an average size of 37" from the ground to the tip of its shoulder and 6' from nose to end of its hairless tail. It has razor-sharp yellow incisors and beady black eyes perfectly adapted for seeing underground. They are fortified with a dense outer membrane of long, oily black fur, allowing it to be mildly protected from edged weapons, which also makes them slightly less pervious to injury from poison or venom. Their main natural enemy is the vipercon and yellow scorpions. However, they have no useful biological appendages to be exploited by any other species. Common weapons used in defense are its four-inch incisors. It is well adapted to life inside caves and rarely spotted out in the light of day unless it is cornered or starving. Diet; Small insects, flesh of any consistency, fruits, and fond of moldy bread. Notable Attributes; They survive by scavenging and can be slightly domesticated for the use of transporting Norgons. They are highly aggressive and will attack anything that wanders too close.

GREEN ENTITY;

Highly mutated biological entity species of unknown origin and size with no identifiable skin or skeletal structure. A gelatinous green and slightly luminescent creature that excretes a sweet honey-scented poisonous gas to lure its prey. Its body consists of an oozing and slimy substance which can conform to any shape or size. It also has the ability to excrete a highly acidic substance to dissolve and digest its prey when it collapses. Diet; Meat or any protein-based substance. Notable Attributes; It is only found inside caves and caverns and is highly responsive to vibrations, and it appears to be unable to relocate from its surroundings once it takes root in an area.

LIFE LEACH;

A simple and unevolved life form that can grow to over 6' in length from tip of mouth to tail once fully fed. Covered with a thick fleshy outer membrane with no identifiable skeletal structure and is easily penetrated with edged weapons when its hide is moist and fresh. It has six bright yellow eyes perfectly adapted for seeing in murky water. Their main natural enemy is the pacu fish and the razor-nosed shark. However, their hide is extremely valuable and is exploited by many sentient species because when it is properly cured, it will transform into an iron-like material. Common weapons used in its defense are its multiple rows of razor-sharp green teeth that can quickly rotate in a clockwise direction. Although it does not have any other viable weapons for defense, it is well-adapted hunt in swamps and marshy areas. Diet; Any creature it can lock its jaws into. It will drain all the blood and life force from its prey quickly and leave only a dried-up husk behind. Notable Attributes; These creatures are fast-moving and swim in large schools, and never leave the water due to the fact that even the shortest exposure to sunlight will cause their hide to harden.

RAPTOIDS;

A highly developed subterranean insect species averaging between 1/2" to 9" tall from the ground to the tip of its shoulder and well adapted with eight legs and fangs ranging up to three inches in length. Six small cold black eyes wrapping around the circumference of their heads capable of seeing 180° and perfectly adapted for seeing underground. They are fortified with a thin outer membrane of an exoskeleton that is as clear as glass in midlevel light and is highly resistant to poison tip arrow. Their main natural enemies are the yellow scorpion and the green entity. They have no useful biological appendages or properties exploitable by any other species. Common weapons used is its stealth and a highly venomous bite which is ten times more potent drop for drop than a vipercon. It is well adapted to life inside caves and are never spotted out in light of day due to having no pigment in their exoskeleton; they will burst into flames on the first contact of sunlight. Diet; Small insects, small to medium-sized game, and expectably fond of nonvertebrate insects and worms. Notable Attributes; Feared by everything that lives in the caves due to its inability to be seen before they strike. Their young may be as small as a pebble; however, they can grow to be as large as a desert cat and kill a full-grown rinog with a single bite if it can penetrate into soft tissue. They are highly aggressive, move and hunt in swarms and will attack anything that moves in their vicinity.

RINOG;

A subset of the Rinosaurur-Saevus species averaging 6' to 10' tall from the tip of its pointy gray horns to the ground. They are fortified with a grey and dense, fleshy outer membrane, which is highly resistant to edged weapons and poison tip arrows. Its head resembles a common prehistoric rhinoceros with two extremely sturdy horns growing to an average length of 9". Two beady red eyes not adapted well for low light areas, two strong club-like hands, and its breath smells like sulfur. Their main natural enemies are the vipercon species, dragons, and the green entity. However, their hide is extremely valuable and is exploited by many sentient species to be used as armor plating as well as their horns are sought after for medicinal purposes. It is well adapted to life inside The Shadow Forest and the subterranean worlds. Diet; Scavenger by trait but will eat any creature it can catch or graze on any vegetation. Notable Attributes; Known to be the worst-tempered creature on the planet and will not hesitate to impose its will on other creatures by brute force, and it is also known to steal for pleasure.

ZINTAR;

A subterranean city populated by approximately 58,000 Zintarian reptiloid species as well as 14,000 various other sentient species. Located deep within The Shadow Forest and buried approximately ½ mile under the Great Crystal Mountain. The city is well fortified with tall stone walls spanning the width of a large cavern, and its entrance is secured with highly decorated large iron gates. The light most commonly used are large torches and the occasional mounted star crystals along the streets and against buildings where a torch would be unsafe to burn. The creatures that inhabit within its walls reside in stone block housing structures that can accommodate one to five "family units" on each level. Located in the center of the city and close to the fresh stream of water diverted from an underground river is a stone castle. This structure is used for public gatherings, a storage facility for food distribution, and it is the home of their sovereign leader, Queen Lylah. Notable Attributes; The Zintarian race has a more defined social, economic, and political infrastructure than the Norgon Race. The Zintarians are allowed to choose their professions and vote for their Queen or King to rule over them. However, in a case of a disputed outcome, the two proposed rulers would have to fight to the death for the honor of serving the people of Zintar. The Zintarians also have a very deep-seated faith in the relationship between their ancestors and themselves. This faith structure is directed and taught by the oldest members of the Zintarian race who maintain a high place in their political and sociological sects and are referred to as "The Elders." Since the great divide between the Norgon and Zintarian societies, the Zintarians had to resort to minimizing their plantings and crops to only growing a starchy edible bulb close to the potato plant and some vined fruit. They had also adapted their crop yields by utilizing the leafy vegetation into a mulch where they could harvest insects and grubs.

NOTEWORTHY INSIGHT;

BLUE FIRE RUBIES;

Highly valuable crystalline structures that are extremely valuable and are exploited by many sentient species. In the dim light, the crystals will emit a soft glowing light that will appear to swirl from the widest part of the crystal in a clockwise direction until it flickers out like a flame at the uppermost point of the crystal. This light will get more vibrant when a storm approaches or when it is warmed slightly by holding it. The age and strength of the crystal can be measured by the intensity and color of the light. The older and stronger the crystal is, the brighter and deeper the color will become. These crystals are very rare, and its vibrational properties can be quite effective in medicinal applications to heal or cure diseases when properly administered.

MEET DAVID WALKER

David Walker has a staggering imagination and is not afraid to use it. He lives with his wife of over 25 years, has 4 kids, 6 grandkids and a completely insane dog. Poppy Dave will take every opportunity to do some Walking Dead couch surfing instead of watching some lame new cartoons. The thing he loves the most is at bed time, asking the kids; present, past, or future? Real or make-believe? With these two little questions, his imagination will be released, sending everyone spiraling into the heart of the mind-blowing realms of the incredible. So, what are you waiting for? Grab some popcorn and join them as they venture into this treacherous world of The Shadow Forest!

COBASFANG'S QUEST IS NOT OVER.
THERE IS SO MUCH MORE
HE HAS TO DO.

SO GET READY FOR HIS
ADVENTURE TO CONTINUE IN
VOLUME 2.

THE ADVENTURES OF
COBASFANG RAID ON NORGON
CITY!

(Volume 2)

Printed in the USA
CPSIA information can be obtained
at www.ICGtesting.com
JSHW011910210724
66591JS00004B/14